# FLIGHT

## EDITED BY
## MATT SINCLAIR

Elephants Bookshelf Press
Springfield, N.J.

Matt Sinclair/Elephant's Bookshelf Press
P.O. Box 214
Summit, N.J. 07902
publisher@elephantsbookshelfpress.com
www.elephantsbookshelfpress.com

Publisher's Note: This is a work of fiction. Names, characters, places, and incidents are a product of the author's imagination. Locales and public names are sometimes used for atmospheric purposes. Any resemblance to actual people, living or dead, or to businesses, companies, events, institutions, or locales is completely coincidental.

Book Layout ©2017 BookDesignTemplates.com

Ordering Information:
Quantity sales. Special discounts are available on quantity purchases by corporations, associations, and others. For details, contact the "Special Sales Department" at the address above.

Flight/ Matt Sinclair -- 1st ed.
ISBN 978-1-940180-92-2 (paperback)
ISBN 978-1-940180-93-9 (e-book)

*Anthologies from Elephant's Bookshelf Press*

–SPRING FEVERS (2012)
–THE FALL (2012)
–SUMMER'S EDGE (2013)
–SUMMER'S DOUBLE EDGE (2013)
–WINTER'S REGRET (2014)
–TALES FROM THE BULLY BOX (2014)
–HORRORS: REAL, IMAGINED, AND DEADLY (2015)


*Novels from Elephant's Bookshelf Press*

–WHISPERING MINDS, BY A.T. O'CONNOR (2013)
–BATTERY BROTHERS BY STEVEN CARMAN (2014)
–BILLY BOBBLE MAKES A MAGIC WAND BY R.S. MELLETTE (2014)
–BILLY BOBBLE AND THE WITCH HUNT BY R.S. MELLETTE (2016)
–LOST WINGS BY DON M. VAIL (2017)


*Nonfiction from Elephant's Bookshelf Press*

–WHICH THE DAYS NEVER KNOW: A YEAR IN VIETNAM
BY THE NUMBERS
BY DONALD MCNAMARA (2018)

# Contents

# INTRODUCTION

I enjoy completing crossword puzzles. They're good for exercising the brain and keeping it flexible.

It's not just the challenge of filling every box that appeals to me. I appreciate a well-constructed puzzle. I like how the constructor weaves in a theme to guide (and occasionally frustrate) the person trying to solve the puzzle.

The clues are part of the game. You learn quickly: one word can have multiple meanings.

In a sense, that's what was behind the overarching theme of this collection of short stories. From the beginning of EBP, I knew I wanted to put together a science fiction anthology. It was one of the first genre ideas we had at the launch of Elephant's Bookshelf Press.

But when putting together such an anthology, it isn't enough just to seek out authors of science fiction. We wanted something more.

When one of my writer friends suggested the idea of *flight* for this anthology, it immediately clicked with me, like when I figure out the answer to a well-written clue in a crossword.

Indeed, once the stories came in, I realized "flight" had even more meanings, more possibilities, than I had ever considered.

Of course, there is space flight in this collection, but R.S. Mellette also pits drag racers in vehicles flying across the country. Death-bringers tangle on winged steeds above the plains of Iowa in Kel Heinen's delightful contribution, "Death's Auction." And Robert Wayne McCoy's story includes a flight of beers in a bizarre power struggle (that involves a rather sick sock). And in perhaps the oddest story we selected, Jon Fried's "Primary Season (Love Red on Planet Blue)," the flight taking place is a somewhat existential departure from confined comfort zones. After all, there are myriad answers to the question of why the chicken crossed the road.

Another question that was always in my mind as we read the submissions was *Is it science fiction?*

To be honest, I suspect some of our decisions will leave you wondering the same thing. As a longtime lover of the genre, I take a somewhat liberal view in answering that question. To me, science fiction includes the realm of the Twilight Zone, where astounding things can and will occur.

I'd love to hear from you, whether you agree or not, about the stories we included. Because we have more science fiction in the hopper. At the end of the anthology, you'll have a chance to get a taste of the next novel from Elephant's Bookshelf Press: *Dark Star Warrior: The Morian Treasure.*

In launching the Dark Star Warrior series, R.S. Mellette introduces us to an amazing universe of space pirates and diplomats. After all, what could possibly go wrong when you mix them together?

We'd love to have you sign up to receive updates on our upcoming titles and the wide array of EBP authors and their stories, which we're excited to introduce to you. We have a lot more in store for you, and the way time flies, these books will be ready before you know it!

# RAP.T.O.R.: RAPID TRANSGLOBAL ORGANIZED RACING

## R.S. MELLETTE

Connor Jenkins took his head in both hands and twisted it to crack his neck. The race would start any minute and he was trying hard not to absorb the nervous tension surrounding him. He flexed his shoulders a bit. His muscles ached from a morning workout, but he liked it that way; it made him feel stronger than his fifteen years. Legally, he wasn't allowed to drive a regular car, much less a flying RAPTOR. Of course, there was nothing legal about underground racing. Connor used that to his advantage. No one saw his face. No one knew who he was. In legit RAPTOR, that would be strange, but it was common in the illegal circuit.

Months ago, Connor had stolen a flame-retardant flight suit and spray-painted it black. To the hood, he stitched in reflective swimming goggles. He could see out, no one could see in. He called himself "Shadow Count." As he shook out his hands and feet, he couldn't help but smile at the thought of the sleaze-ball signing him in as a pilot for the first time nine months ago. "Shadow Count!? Where'd that stupid handle come from?"

Connor had kept it cool. "Count Zero was taken." The sleazeball didn't get it; obviously not a Gibson fan.

Today, Shadow Count was no longer a stupid handle. Still in his rookie year, Connor had made it out of the pit and flown well in two races. Most rookies landed in the hospital more often than in a driver's seat. Anyone good enough to make it out of the pit either died in his first race or his next visit to the pit. Shadow Count was now the handle of a pilot who had earned some measure of respect.

Of the myriad and ever-changing rules to underground RAPTOR racing, the one Connor liked most was the fight for cars. Any pilot who wanted to enter this illegal, dangerous, event could, whether they owned a car or not. Most didn't. Sure, some rich pricks built their own so they could skip the pit, stay clean, uninjured, and get a massive head start. The rest, like Connor, weren't so privileged.

The game was simple. At the sound of the starting gun, get out of the mosh pit, into a car, and go. Then try to catch up to the rich pricks. The problem was fifty other pilots wanted to do the same thing, and there were no rules about how they got to do it.

The sponsors – a collection of people well-off enough and criminal enough to put up money for this blood sport – watched, laughed, and bet on everything from who would get what car, to how many bones would be broken. Their leader, Johnny Santos, looked down on the pilots the way a Roman Emperor might despise his gladiator-slaves. His contempt was particularly irritating to Connor, since Johnny was just three years older. That was far too young in Connor's mind to have such power. Connor didn't know Jack Santos, Johnny's father, but was told he had been respected, as much as one can respect the head of an illegal syndicate. Since Senior's criminal conviction and long sentence, Johnny had been running things, which was a big complaint among the pilots.

Connor tried his best not to care about the dark side of the Santos family. They ran the sport, and the car fight had almost all he needed to make him happy – almost. Outside of the pit were the cars, some brand new and gleaming, others battle-worn and weary. All of them were expensive, so far out of reach of Connor's world that they might as well have been on the moon. Still, Connor loved them. No matter what the condition or the price, everything about a RAPTOR car said speed to him— dangerous, angry, speed. Like a shark or a jet fighter, there was something undeniably attractive about the RAPTOR lines, air-intakes, propulsion systems, and weapons. They wanted to run, just like Connor. They were angry, just like Connor. And they needed a pilot like Connor.

Inside the pit, he got to do the other thing that made him happy: hit people. He didn't know why that made him feel better. It shouldn't. Worse still, he didn't know why getting hit made him nearly as happy as hitting. Mostly he didn't care why. He did it to get to a car. Liking it was just a bonus.

Connor staked out the middle of the mosh pit. Next to him stood a guy twice his size and age but half his experience. Connor knew that because the idiot was crowding him before the start. Around them, Connor recognized about twenty pilots he knew to be seasoned. They kept at least an arm's distance from everyone else and stayed light on their toes.

Several of the veterans glanced back at Connor and the big burly guy dumb enough to stand so close. A pilot Connor had seen around before caught his eye. No one had friends in the pit, but common enemies sometimes made for allies. The pilot pointed to Connor, then put his thumb up and raised an eyebrow. It was a question. "Are you okay with the big guy?"

Connor pretended to scratch his elbow, revealing to his new associate a knife blade hidden in his protective pad. The other pilot smiled. Connor shrugged as if to say, "Pilot's gonna do what a pilot's gotta do."

Around the edges of the pit stood mostly rookies. Their strategy was to be closest to the wall at the start, hoping to climb it quicker than the pilot next to them could pull them down. It rarely worked.

Connor didn't think about the race. Not yet. If he didn't get a car, he wouldn't get to race. He did try to block out the smells and ugliness that surrounded him. Besides the pilots, who were not known for their personal hygiene, the warehouse overflowed with the scum of high society. They loved rubbing elbows with the dangerous set, even if the biggest dangers they faced were watered down drinks. They reveled in the desperation of the competitors who were a mix of young up-and-comers like Connor, ex-pros who couldn't give up their adrenaline addiction, and desperation jocks hoping to make enough money to survive. Connor tried not to think about how he might belong to that last set. Instead, he focused on Johnny, waiting for him to signal the fat fart on stage with the starting gun.

There would be no "ready, set, go." Johnny would give a little nod and the fat guy would fire when he felt like it. Connor watched so closely because he needed to cheat without getting caught.

Johnny tossed his head up ever so slightly. The fat fart raised his gun. A millisecond before the start, Connor slammed his elbow under the chin of the idiot pilot who had been crowding him. The sound of his breaking jaw was blocked out by the bang of the starting pistol. From the blood that sprayed out of his mouth, Connor figured his blade found its mark. That, or the idiot bit off his tongue. Either way, Connor was in for a soggy race.

He grabbed his victim's head like a bowling ball, with a thumb in his mouth and two fingers in the new hole under his jaw, put a foot in the guy's chest and roll him over in a backward summersault, kicking him out at the end. His upside-down body knocked over four other fighters, clearing a path for Connor to make a run for the wall.

One guy took advantage of that path, but Connor clocked him in the ear from behind without missing a step. The rookies fighting close to the wall had piled on top of each other the way they always did. Connor ran up their backs and out of the pit.

About thirty others were out and running toward the cars. Most headed for the newest and shiniest of them. *Idiots,* thought Connor. He ran for one of the older, beaten-up vehicles. Only one pilot was ahead of him, climbing into the saddle. Connor grabbed him and felt something he wasn't used to: hips.

He pulled the woman off the car, spun her around, and would have punched her lights out, but her lights – her eyes – were so beautiful. No older than his, they were the only thing he could see of her, as she was disguised in a flight suit like his, but they were enough to stop his fist. For one brief second, Connor saw the fear in her. He also saw her clean skin, what little of it showed. She wasn't covered in grease, sweat, and the dirt of illegal RAPTOR racing. She seemed out of place in Connor's world.

Instead of hitting her, he glanced over to the next car. One guy was in the saddle, not strapped in, struggling with the starter. The girl in Connor's grasp got a hand free and punched him hard in the face. It was a good punch, but pain was never a deterrent for Connor. She cocked her arm to hit him again, but Connor pinned her wrist over her head against the vehicle.

"Take the car," he said before letting her go.

Her eyes widened with surprise. Before she could figure out what had happened, he ran over to the other car and pulled the would-be pilot out of the seat. Connor jumped in and immediately closed the Plexiglas dome. No sooner did he do that than ten more racers jumped on board to try to take his place.

"Lesson one, rookie," said Connor to no one in particular, "close the dome first." He strapped in and fired up the engines. The smart attackers jumped off the car. The dumb ones fell off when Connor shot twenty feet into the air and waggled his wings. He kicked the throttle hard, flying off into the night.

The race was on.

A female voice came over his radio. "Shadow Count, is that you on my six?"

"Not for long," said Connor.

"No worries. I just wanted to say thanks. But don't expect any favors."

"I never do," said Connor.

"Loki out."

*So her name is Loki,* thought Connor. That was all the time he had for social niceties. He kicked on his afterburners and blew by Loki just shy of the sound barrier.

The game that night was follow the leader. Whatever car was in the lead set the course around the planet. Everyone else had to stay within a mile of his horizontal line. Racers could fly higher or lower than the lead, but side-to-side they had to be within a mile of the lead's path.

"Syscom, show me the line."

On his heads-up display, the system computer overlaid a green line. It looked to be a half a mile away to his left, running parallel to his course. Connor had a good start for a pit monkey.

"Syscom, what's my position?"

"You are running fifth, two hundred miles off lead, and fifty miles off fourth."

"Show me fourth."

On his heads-up display a red dot appeared above and ahead of him on the other side of the green line. A red line streaming off the dot indicated its path. "He's running too high," said Connor to himself.

The cardinal rule of underground RAPTOR was that no one broke the sound barrier over a country capable of defending her airspace. This race started in Los Angeles, and the lead headed east, so the speed limit would be Mach .85.

But the higher a car flies, the slower sound travels. Mach .85 at 30,000 feet is slower than it is at sea level. If Connor had the guts to trim the trees all the way to Kansas, he'd move 100 miles an hour faster than the idiot at 40,000. To save fuel, though, he'd have to stay low enough to take advantage of the ground-effect air cushion. That meant he had to fly closer to the ground than his wings were wide – about 25 feet high. At night over a desert, that would quickly become mountains, or a power line, or a tall tree.

"We have a word for pilots who fly the ram," his father once told him.

"Yeah? What's that?"

"Dead."

"Syscom, Radar, visual enhance, tight and close." On the screen, a detailed, multicolor overlay showed the obstacles ahead. Connor eased his car down until he felt it float on the cushion of air between him and the ground. "Syscom, Speed relative to fourth."

Next to the red dot that was the pilot in fourth place a green number appeared, 75 mph. Green meant Connor was gaining. He glanced at his airspeed: Mach .65. He focused on the terrain ahead of him, a long flat desert good for his air cushion, but one set of power lines would end him.

Connor pushed the throttle until the wind over his canopy sounded right. He didn't dare take his eyes off the ground racing toward him to check his speed. "Syscom, speed."

"Mach .85"

Connor smiled. *Nailed it.*

Just then the system computer spoke up again. "New Lead. New heading."

The pilot in second place made a move and was now in first. That meant everyone had to follow that path. The green line on Connor's screen shifted to the right of his position and closer to his dangerously low altitude. A hundred miles ahead of him it turned southeast. *Good*, thought Connor, *He's taking the flat route.*

"Ramming the cushion" as they called the ultra-low strategy required flat land to optimize the fuel. Whoever was in the lead now wanted to avoid the Sierra Nevada and Rocky Mountains. The route would take them along the US/Mexican border and down the Rio Grande basin to the Gulf of Mexico. Connor knew it well.

"Syscom, play the commentary."

A screen on his console turned on, but Connor didn't dare take his eyes off his route. The speakers inside his helmet filled with the online coverage of the underground TUBRO network. "That shift south has put California's favorite pit monkey,

Shadow Count, into fourth place," said the play-by-play announcer.

"The Count has come a long way since his early days, Bob."

Connor had to smile to himself. He was only fifteen and still in his rookie year. These were his early days. Still, they had it right. He'd come a long way.

*"Frank, I don't care about the money! You have to get rid of that car."*

*It wasn't Connor's first memory of his father; it was his last. His parents were fighting, as they often did. His mother wanted his father, a one-time pilot in the Eye circuit, to give up driving. Connor was too young then to know the difference between the legit International RAPTOR Circuit – the "Eye" – and the illegal, underground circuit his father, and now Connor, ended up in. All Connor knew at the time was his Dad raced RAPTORs – and taught him how to do it, too.*

*"That car is killing you," his mother said. They argued in the living room that was also the kitchen. Connor lay in bed. The walls between them might as well have been paper.*

*"It's not the car, Charlotte. We need the money."*

*"Then sell it! Get a different job. There are plenty of jobs in RAPTOR racing, you don't have to be the driver."*

*"Pilot. We're called pilots."*

*"Whatever! Just quit doing it. We need you here at home. Get out of it."*

*"It's too late for that. Once you're in, they don't let you out."*

*Connor heard the front door open and close. He never heard from his father again.*

On the horizon, Connor saw the flash of a vapor cone. That had to be the car ahead of him going transonic, so near the speed of sound that parts of the flying car would break the barrier depending on air pressure and temperature. To Connor it meant they'd reached the US-Mexican border. There was an unspoken agreement between US Homeland Security, Fuerza Aérea Mexicana, and illegal RAPTOR racers. So long as no one complained, they kept speeds below the sound barrier, and clearly identified as RAPTOR cars, neither country would intercept them along the border.

Connor pushed his speed up to Mach .9.

*"To be a RAPTOR driver," his father told him the first time they got in a car together, "you have to use your head. You have to know when friction is good and bad. You have to know about lift versus drag and all about aerodynamics."*

*"How did you learn that?" he asked his father.*

*"Experience," he said, "Now listen. You also have to be in good physical shape. If you get caught in a dive, your life just might depend on your ability to pull back on the stick against G-forces that make you feel like you weigh six times your normal weight."*

*Connor did the math. He weighed a little less than a hundred pounds then. Six hundred pounds! How is that possible?*

*His father must have seen the look on his face. "Don't worry. You get used to it."*

*"Are you going to teach me how to drive?"*

*"I'm going to teach you everything, son."*

*Connor's father was as good as his word. He taught his son everything he could as long as he was around, which wasn't long enough as far as Connor was concerned.*

Connor closed in on the third-place car. He armed his rockets, though both pilots knew he wouldn't fire anywhere over North America. He also raised his altitude to five thousand feet.

*"It's not like drafting behind a car on the ground." Connor and his father sat next to each other in their apartment, wearing virtual reality headsets running a RAPTOR flight simulator.*

*His Dad taught the lesson. "Hang on, I'll make the turbulence visible."*

*Connor could see his virtual father's hands flip a switch on the virtual controls in front of him. The simulated RAPTOR car flying ahead disappeared behind red swirling winds coming off each wingtip.*

*"Those things that look like sideways tornadoes are called 'wake turbulence' and they are as strong as real tornadoes. Since we're in a simulator, and we can't die, let's do what you should never, ever do. Get right behind that lead car."*

*Connor tried to do as he was told, but as he got closer to the lead car, he lost control. The down blast from the wingtip vortex smashed them into the ground.*

*"And we're dead," said his father.*

Back in his RAPTOR car, Connor wondered if that's how his father actually died.

❁

Two sonic booms rumbled way ahead of Connor. That would be the lead and second place cars going supersonic over the international waters of the Gulf. The third car had fallen so far behind the first two that Connor figured he either had engine trouble or didn't have the guts for the fast and low path being taken.

A third option might be that he was laying a trap for Connor. He eased off the throttle to stay behind third place.

"Syscom, check my six." Connor could have looked at the scope himself, but he kind of wanted someone to talk to.

"Radar is clear behind us."

That meant no one within two hundred miles, but they were back there. "Syscom, put the commentary on again."

His headset filled with sound from back at the warehouse and the two online narrators of the race. "Vapor Shock is true to his handle, Bob. He's put the pedal down, ramping up to Mach 7 over the Gulf with Sonic Sam right on his tail."

"They'll be in Cuba in a few minutes, but the real race now is for third. What do you think is up with the Killer? His speed is down to Mach .6. Is he in trouble?"

"I don't think so. He sees there's a pit monkey on his six and they don't call him the Killer for nothing. If that pilot passes him over the Gulf, he'll be shot down before he hits Mach 1."

"Do you think the Killer knows that's Shadow Count?"

Connor couldn't believe it. *He does now, you idiots.*

Sure enough, Killer kicked his speed up to Mach .9. Connor kept pace.

"Just tell me who's behind me," said Connor as if the commentators could hear him.

Apparently, they did. "Five hundred miles behind Shadow Count, Loki leads the rest of the pit monkey pack."

"What do we know about him, Bob?"

"Only that he's a she, and she's a rookie. This is the first time she's made it out of the pit."

"It'll be fun to see how she handles herself."

Ahead of Connor, Killer slowed to nearly stalling speed. The fight was on.

*"Sometimes slower is better."*

*Connor remembered his first dogfight lesson with his dad. They both wore virtual reality headsets, but this time they were in different cars. They flew side-by-side. His dad kept slowing down.*

*"Don't let me get behind you," he said.*

*Connor's virtual controls all flashed red. Stall warnings buzzed. "I can't go any slower."*

*"Then you have to figure out how to go fast and get behind me."*

Connor rammed the throttle forward and pulled the stick into his lap. He barked against the G-forces pulling on his body. When he saw Mother Earth directly overhead, he popped a snap-roll. That Immelmann maneuver put him upright on a heading 180 degrees from where he started.

Below, Killer banked into a hard turn as he tried to circle around to regain his position.

A woman's voice came over his com. "Count, Loki. You okay?"

"I'm fine. You've got two targets in front of you. I'm not asking any favors, but... you know."

Red lights flashed in his cockpit. "MISSLE LAUNCH," screamed the mechanical voice.

Connor checked his scope.

"Okay, we're even," said Loki.

Sure enough, her missile headed toward Killer. He fired chaff, turned tail, and ran toward the ocean, his vapor cone and chaff visible to Connor before the thunder of his sonic boom.

Connor turned to get back on his original heading, when Loki hailed him. "I told you not to expect any favors."

"MISSILE LAUNCH!"

Connor fired chaff and slammed the stick into his right thigh, but it was no use. The missiles exploded with a near-field electro-magnetic pulse, killing everything electrical on his bird.

*"It looks like Shadow is down for the count."*

Without propulsion he went weightless as his car fell like a rock toward the Louisiana coast. Waiting for drag to slow him down to terminal velocity, he wondered; should he be angry or impressed with the mysterious girl who shot him down?

If he didn't eject before the car deployed its Mars-Rover-like airbags, he'd be bounced to death inside the car. If he ejected too soon, the concussion of air at that speed would kill him, so he waited in the high G-force of a flat spin, with his hands firmly on the manual eject lever.

"Loki?" He tried to keep his voice cool between the "hut-hut" noises he had to make to keep from blacking out. "You're true to your name."

"Thanks." She sounded like she was on a lazy summer stroll. "You can buy me a drink when you get back to LA."

"That's..." *hut-hut* "...a date." He'd have to figure out how to get a fake ID before then, but that was the least of his problems.

There would be no warning light. No speed indicators. Without electricity, he just had to guess when to eject. The syndicate didn't care if he died in the crash. They just wanted their car back.

When he could see the horizon over the dash, he pulled the lever. Two shotgun shells blew the canopy off and a pair of rockets blasted him clear of the ship. He lost consciousness just long enough to miss the jaw-crunching jerk of the chutes catching air.

When he came to, still floating to the ground, he thought, *At least Mom will like Loki, 'cause she got me to stop racing... for now.*

# THE LOVER'S FLIGHT

## N.B. TURNER

The man managed about two feet of lift before the explosion ripped him apart. Blood burned into the test pad soil, and spectators covered their ears against the blast. Smoldering flesh landed underneath the warden's observation platform, next to the charred remains of other test pilots.

"There goes test number seven," Peter, the prison warden, said. He slammed his boot into the railing, before turning his scowl to Elijah.

Elijah cursed. "The idiot didn't control the fuel intake, I bet. Let too much in and turned the thing into a bomb."

"Was it the pilot or the designer?" The warden barked. "You bragged that you could build this machine. So do it!"

"I'm trying!" Elijah protested.

"Try harder. Or maybe I need to turn up that speaker in your cell."

"No! I'll have another test in two days. I'll get it right!"

"See that you do." Peter stepped inside the elevator and left the observation platform, sliding smoothly down the metal tube.

Elijah's feet skidded across the platform and down the stairs as the guards took him back to his cell. He was in no hurry. He knew what awaited him there.

His cell was cramped: a cot chained to the wall, a hole in the floor for bodily functions, a window wide enough to check the weather, and a speaker controlled in Peter's office. Once inside, he heard the speaker buzz and click. The first slap rang through the box; the whip cracked and stung Elijah's ears. Banging against the bars didn't help drown out the screaming: his beloved Emily, far beyond sight, was begging *"Stop! Please!"*

The warden's voice shot through the speaker: "Elijah, have you figured out what you did wrong? Have you found the flaw in the machine yet?"

The whip cracked again. *"Mercy..."* Emily always begged, but Peter would only hit harder when she did. Her words soon turned to whimpers, screams, and tears. Elijah sobbed with each crack of the whip, which he could picture slashing across her skin. He couldn't plead or beg like her: he knew it wouldn't stop until he finally perfected the machine.

Dawn broke across Elijah's eyes the next morning. The speaker was silent. He heard gulls cawing over the open ocean through the cell window.

He rose from the cot and landed his shackle-scarred feet in their well-worn places on the floor. Emily's screams rang in his ears: nightmares of her contorted face had plagued his sleep. Smacking himself on the head, he tried to knock the sound loose. *Concentrate,* he thought. *You need to concentrate. You need to fix the machine.*

Keys rattled beside the cell door. Elijah saw Sancho, the blind and curious guard, fiddle with the ring and slip the key into the lock. "Elijah," he said. "It's time for you to go to the workshop again."

"I know, Sancho," Elijah said. He pounded his palm three times against the metal frame before he left the cot; the deep bone pain helped him awaken. Elijah left the cell and Sancho was behind him, more like a boy following an uncle than a guard following a prisoner.

Sancho extended his arm and dragged his callused knuckles against the walls as he walked. When the wall ran out, he announced a turn: left, right, right. Sancho's knuckles knew every crack in the wall, his feet knew each uneven stone. He was the perfect guard: sharp enough to hear everything, too blind to see beauty outside the prison. The island prison was home, and Sancho was told to make sure that he kept his guests inside.

Elijah silently cursed the chains on his feet once more: he could outrun Sancho if he could just stretch his legs. But each time Sancho announced a turn Elijah had forgotten, or found himself confused in the damp prison halls, Elijah remembered that the place was meant to be a maze. Prisoners could run from Sancho, but they would starve within its walls. Peter kept a complete map; some guards had sections of maps for the area they controlled. Only Sancho knew the place by heart.

They reached the workshop and Sancho swung the door open. Elijah shuffled inside, turned to Sancho, and waited for his chains to be released. Work was the only time he was free of chains. Sancho fumbled the key into the hole and the cuffs sloughed off Elijah's wrists; the shackles remained on his feet. Sancho slamming the door shut was his signal to start working.

Pieces of Elijah's last design were scattered on the worktable. Each failed test required a mechanical autopsy. Charred metal shards and fractured tank walls confirmed his first guess: a valve had come loose from the fuel intake mechanism. Without regulating fuel, the machine had turned itself into a bomb. *Tighter screws,* he thought. *Or better welds?* He grabbed sheet metal from the corner and started working it in the vises.

"What was wrong with it?" Sancho asked when Elijah paused. He kept his ear plastered to the cell door tray slot, listening to

Elijah's hammer and torch work the metal sheets into a shape he couldn't see.

"Can't tell you, Sancho," Elijah said.

"What can you tell me?"

"Would you like to hear a story?"

"You know I love stories." Elijah heard a shuffling and imagined Sancho sitting by the door, waiting for Elijah's voice. "What is it this time?"

"It's about a man who tries to conquer an enemy without fighting him."

Stories were how Elijah entertained the blind man-child "watching" him. A poor bastard, under Peter's care, Sancho was forced to guard the wretched prisoners; a story was the least Elijah could do for him. Between hammer blows, he told the story: "So, the man brings a rose to his enemy—"

"What's a rose?" Sancho said, interrupting as he tended to do when he was confused.

"A flower. Red. Thorny."

*So many questions,* Elijah thought. He answered as many as he could. Storytelling was the only time Elijah found his sight to be a problem. *How do I explain something to someone who lacks the main sense I use?*

A few hours later, Elijah announced that he was done. Sancho stood up and rattled the keys. Elijah stood in the open door and gave the groping Sancho his hands. Iron cuffs slammed shut, cutting the edge of his wrists.

Sancho paused when Elijah gasped. "Did I hurt you, Elijah?"

"You scraped me up a bit, Sancho," he said, blood trickling down his wrist to his fingertips.

"I'm sorry!" Fumbling fingers stuffed a dirty rag underneath the cuffs, staunching the blood. "How is the work going?"

"Fine," Elijah said. "Sorted out the last problem."

"Will you ever tell me why you're working on this machine?"

"Maybe one day, Sancho. When it's finished." Sancho extended his knuckles to the wall and started navigating back to Elijah's cell. An evening meal awaited the inventor, along with Peter.

"Evening, Sancho," Peter said.

"Evening, sir," Sancho said. He bowed his head and Peter's hand stroked his hair.

"Would you leave Elijah with me, please?"

"Of course." Sancho handed the keys over and left the two alone.

Elijah watched the guard traipse off before Peter yanked him inside by the chains. Peter stood against the brick wall, stretching his chain-free legs; Elijah sat on his bed, revolted by the slop before him. "Eat," Peter said. "You'll need it to keep working."

"I've fixed it, ok? It should work now."

"You said that last time."

"Your pilot was the problem. I've told you that I need to teach them how to work it before they test it. Or better yet, you let me try it out."

"Or you could just draw your blueprints up and let my scientists build it."

"I told you that I can't draw them," Elijah lied. "I have to build it from memory."

"Whatever. I hope for Emily's sake—"

"It's not her fault! You're the one keeping her locked up. You can let her go whenever you want."

"Not until you finish the machine." Peter pulled a cigarette from his pocket and struck a match against the wall. A long drag burned a quarter of it to ash.

"What are you here for?"

"I always come to see you after a failure. Try to see how you're doing. We were once cordial, weren't we?"

"Once." From the tray, Elijah grabbed a spoon and pressed his thumb into its bowl. He needed something in his hands; Peter's neck wasn't an option. "After you shoved me into this prison, it's hard to call you a friend."

"I asked for your assistance. You wouldn't provide it willingly. I had no other option. Your machine can do a lot of things that I need."

"It could also provide a lot of things I need."

"Then why can't you help me?"

"Because you want to use it to start a war."

"Not start a war. Win one. Imagine what your machine could do. Small, mobile, able to attack where the enemy isn't expecting, agile enough to avoid any defenses they point at the sky. All those nations' riches ours for the taking after we've won."

"It's not meant for that. It was meant to help someone."

"War brings change. Sorely needed change. War could help thousands of people in the end. What's a few deaths compared to that?"

"It won't stop at a few."

"With your machine, it might. Strike the right places, our enemies will crumble."

"Your enemies. Not mine. You're a fool to think it will work like that."

Peter took another drag and burned the cigarette down. He chucked it out the cell window. "Be that as it may, I have Emily. And I don't think she's doing too well."

Elijah's thumb bent the spoon's head backwards.

"I know you don't trust me. But I'm not a liar. Finish the machine. And you two can go free." Peter closed the cell door as he left.

Keys rattled as Peter placed them into Sancho's hands. "Any instructions for the evening?" he asked Peter.

"No. Just keep an eye on him, ok? I want to make sure he's all right."

"But I can't see…"

"I know, Sancho. It's a figure of speech."

"Yes sir."

The blind guard lounged just outside of Elijah's cell, settling into his usual position: out of sight, but never out of earshot. A racket of chains and silverware made Sancho jump. Walls and floor vibrated when Elijah kicked at the base of the cell bars. "Son of a bitch!"

"Who are you talking to?"

"No one, Sancho." Elijah assumed Sancho reported everything to Peter, either under orders or from being so guileless. Eyes being useless, he knew Sancho's ears would be stronger. Elijah didn't even whisper around Sancho unless he wanted Peter to hear it. But Sancho's innocence could be handy. He could ask questions, and Sancho wouldn't know what to lie about. "Do you ever go into the cellar, Sancho?"

"Sometimes."

"Do you ever find anything strange? Like another prisoner?"

"Sometimes. There's a woman down there."

"Have you ever spoken to her?"

"No."

"Do you know anything about her?"

"She sings. Softly."

"What does she sing?"

Sancho tried to sing her melody, but couldn't. He mumbled her words:

*I must away now, I can no longer tarry*
*This morning's tempest, I have to cross*

*I must be guided, without a stumble*
*Into the arms I love the most.*

*It's her,* Elijah thought. His remembered laying with her in bed as she sang that song and ran her fingers through his hair. Every night—after he took her from her wheelchair and covered her atrophied legs with a blanket—he would rest his head on her lap and listen to her sing. That song was their lullaby; she had learned it at her mother's knee.

"Sancho, do you know if you'll see her soon?"

"Probably."

Elijah knelt against the bars, enough to peer his eyes out across the halls: no guards coming, only Sancho in sight. "Sancho, can you tell her something the next time you're near her?"

"I'm not supposed to send messages between prisoners."

"This isn't a message. It's just a song. Nothing important."

"What is it?"

Elijah called Sancho closer, and he obeyed. "If I tell you, you must keep it secret, ok?"

"Ok," he said. Asking anything of Sancho was a risk, but he had to take it. He needed to know if she was still alive.

"Can you tell her this?

*And when he came to his true love's dwelling,*

*He knelt down gently upon a stone*

*And through her window, he whispered lowly*

*Is my true love within at home?*

"Can you say it back to me?"

Sancho repeated the song, once, twice, three times. "Do I have it?"

"Yes, Sancho. Just tell her that." He rattled his hands against the bars, asking Sancho to unlock his chains. With his limbs free, he crawled to his bunk. Sancho was repeating the verse as he fell asleep, and Elijah felt the shadow of his home with Emily creep into his dreams.

At dawn the next morning, Elijah was told that he could teach the test pilot how to work the machine. All other tests, he had to deliver written instructions.

The pilot struggled to fit into the harness and complained that his feet couldn't fit in the stirrups. "They're too short," he said. "Did you build this thing for a child?"

"It's designed for someone with much shorter legs." Elijah took care to explain how to ration the fuel intake, correcting the problem from last time.

After the lesson, Elijah took his place, chains and all, next to Peter on the observation platform. Sancho stood behind him, holding his chain like a leash. A question burned in Elijah's mind, overwhelming his anxiety for the test, almost sickening him to hold it down: *Had Sancho delivered the message?* The pilot's countdown snapped his attention back to the testing ground.

"Ignition lit. Fuel burn, steady. Attempting liftoff." Jet fuel scorched the ground; the pilot's feet hovered a few inches above the ground. "Liftoff achieved. Attempting further ascent." Steady hand on the control, his index finger pressed the button. A few more inches.

"More lift!" Peter said.

"It can't handle that," Elijah shouted. "It will break apart if you push it too hard."

More fuel for the fire: several more inches. "More!" Peter said, ignoring Elijah.

"I don't think I can get higher, sir," the pilot replied, voice shaking through the microphone.

"More lift! Higher!"

The pilot shook his head. He took a deep breath and pressed the button flat. He rose another foot before the blast rattled through the dome and new blood splattered across old scorch marks.

Peter grabbed Elijah's restraints and threw him to the dirt. A rubber boot sole crushed Elijah's scalp, gravel worked into his ear. "What the fuck is wrong with your machine? It's not the pilot this time. You taught him! Maybe it's the design."

"It's working as designed," Elijah spat. His lips scraped dirt into his gums. He spat it out once Peter removed his foot.

"Then why can't they fly?"

"They are. Just not as high as you want. This machine wasn't meant to shoot them into the stratosphere."

"Then fix it so it can. Another test in two days."

"I'll need more time. You're asking me to change the entire design."

Peter's steel-toed boot broke three of Elijah's teeth. "Two days."

Sancho picked up Elijah and dragged him to the cell. Soon, the screaming started again: Emily begging for mercy; Elijah pounding at the bars; Peter telling them both that this was the price of failure. Sancho covered his ears and whispered for them all to stop it.

After Peter had exhausted himself with the whip, Elijah cried himself to sleep. His final waking thought was of Emily in her wheelchair, looking up at a cliff face by their home. They had climbed it as children; Elijah had often climbed it as an adult, while Emily had been bed-ridden after an accident paralyzed her legs. She was so beautiful, but so sad in her chair.

On a whim, he asked, "Would you like to climb it?"

"Oh, yes," she said. "I miss the wind in my face at the top." That was when he decided to build the machine. The moment taunted him now, as if to shame him for his kindness toward her. If he had been cruel, or simple-minded, then she could have been spared all this pain. But instead, he built the machine for her.

He saw Emily flying beside him as he climbed the cliff. She smiled, her slender and tender fingers calmly working the dial and control stick, her shriveled and atrophied legs resting in the stirrups. He found another hold and advanced to the summit, glancing back to her to see that she was rising with him. Hold by hold, foot by foot, they ascended to the top. At the summit, Emily started laughing. The wind was in her face, and Elijah thought she looked like a child again.

Then she screamed, the sound shrill and tortured. Her hand slipped from the controls. Elijah stood on the precipice, watching her plummet toward the earth. "Pull up! Use the throttle! Emily!"

He woke from the dream when she crashed in a fireball. "A bad omen," he said to himself.

When Sancho came to escort him to the workshop, Elijah asked if he had visited the prisoner downstairs.

"Who?" Sancho asked.

"The singing woman. Did you give her the message?" Sancho clapped on the chains and led him to the workshop.

A frightening silence reverberated under the blind guard's dragging knuckles. Each turn exposed Sancho's non-answer. Each time the wall ran on one side, Elijah hoped to hear Sancho speak. Coming to the end of a hall, he stopped, letting the chain go taut.

Tension across his palm made Sancho turn around. "C'mon, Elijah," he said. "Workshop's this way."

"I asked you a question, Sancho," he said. "Answer me."

"I don't want to."

"Answer me, damn it!"

Sancho covered his ears. "Don't scream. Please. I hate the screaming."

Elijah closed his eyes and took a breath. "Then answer me. Please."

Deep snorting forced back the mucus in Sancho's throat. He kept one hand against the wall as he used the hand holding the chain to wipe his eyes. "She's dead. The boss made me carry her outside this morning."

"What?"

"He told me she died in the night. She was so small. Her legs were like sticks."

Elijah collapsed to the floor, rattling the chains and yanking Sancho's hand backward. *She's dead,* he thought. *I couldn't save her.* Iron chafed his skin and opened the cut Sancho had given him two days before. Blood ran across his palm, and smeared his face as he dried his tears. He rose when Sancho pulled on the chain, telling him that the workshop would not wait.

Behind the locked door, free of his chains, Elijah picked up the burnt wreckage of the last design and threw it against the wall. Jagged metal sliced his palms, adding to the blood trickling from his wrists. Another wipe across his crying eyes darkened the red stripe on his face.

A glance at the new metal reflected his face, savage and bloody as an old warrior. An old photo flashed to mind: a soldier on the war path, face marred with a red palm print, described as "ready to avenge his fallen comrades."

Fire and hammer blows took Elijah to midday. When the food slot opened in the door, he heard Sancho sobbing. He sat down with the ration tray, but didn't touch a morsel. He lifted the slot and asked, "Sancho, why are you crying?"

"The woman died," he said. "She was nice to me. She told me stories like you did."

*Emily loved children,* Eljiah thought. *Was Sancho a child to her?* Was. Past tense. Emily was gone, and Peter had taken her from him. And from Sancho, apparently. The crying man-child seemed to demand a story for comfort.

"Would you like to hear a story, Sancho?"

"What kind of a story?"

"A good one. Where the good guy wins and the bad guys lose."

"Yes, please tell me."

"Come close to the door." Elijah went back to work, weaving his tale for Sancho. He told his story: Emily's story. He told of how Peter had heard about Elijah's machine, asked him to build one for him. When he refused, Peter had Elijah and Emily abducted in the middle of the night and brought to this prison. He told of how the first few machines were intentional duds, but then the pilots started failing too. Then Peter started torturing Emily, forcing Elijah to make the machine properly. Finally, he told Sancho, "In the end, the inventor found a way to defeat the warden, but only by sacrificing himself. He knew the warden had to be stopped, to protect people outside the prison."

"What does 'sacrificing himself' mean?" Sancho said.

"The inventor had to die."

"How does that make the good guy win?"

"Because no one else is hurt by the warden. That's what the good guys want."

"But the hero dies."

"Sometimes that has to happen, Sancho."

"Still seems sad."

"Maybe." Elijah took up a pencil and paper from a previously unopened drawer in the work bench. *It needs to be maneuverable,* he thought. *It must catch him by surprise.* He re-designed the nozzle below the fuel tank, adding fins to divert the thrust: it was the last modification he made to the machine.

Peter visited the workshop. "It's late, Elijah. Are you almost done?"

"You're asking me to re-design the entire machine. It takes time." Several hammer thwacks curved sheet metal into a tube. "On that note, the controls have changed a bit. I need to fly this test."

"Why can't you teach a pilot?"

"I can't teach them yet. It won't explode if I make a mistake, but you won't see its full potential unless I fly it."

Elijah waited for Peter to respond. He needed a yes. When it came, he immediately started hammering again. His anger looked like enthusiasm: a tube that had once taken five blows to curve only took two. "Thanks, Peter," he said, but he knew Peter had already left.

"Will you be flying tomorrow, Elijah?" Sancho asked.

"Seems like it."

"I'd like to see that," he said.

*Did he just crack a joke?* Elijah thought, puzzled and yet smiling to himself. *First time for everything, I guess.*

After more hammering, welding, and several rounds of Sancho asking whether he was done, Elijah asked to be led back to his cell. The moon was high in the cell window; midnight, he guessed. Ratcheting the cell door shut no longer scared him, and the final slam, like a nail in a coffin, no longer made him jump.

Sancho unlocked the cuffs and collected the chains once they fell to the ground. "Good night, Elijah," he said, turning to walk away.

"Good night, Sancho." The guard walked away without a pause.

Elijah lay on the cold cot, sleepless. His hands practiced turning the dials, shifting the throttle; his hips practiced shifting his weight to turn and curve at full speed.

Blades of shadow and moonlight crept across the floor, turning to dawn sunlight, which stabbed at Elijah's eyes. He hadn't slept; the sweat-drenched blanket clung to him as he rose.

Sancho bumped into Elijah when he entered the cell. "Sorry about that," he said.

"First time I stood at the door," Elijah said. "Not a problem."

"You excited to fly?"

"Excited enough."

"Is Peter excited?"

"Probably." He didn't wince when Sancho cuffed him. Blood trickled down the familiar canyon and ridges of his hands. *Don't give him any reason to blame himself,* Elijah thought. They started down the familiar path to the testing pad.

Sunlight was beginning to graze the tunnel as Elijah strapped himself into the rig. Behind him, stairs led to the observation platform. Sancho sat on the steps, holding Elijah's chains. *He'll wait until you come back,* Elijah thought. *Just like in the workshop. He'll be out of the way. He'll be safe.* "Be careful, Sancho. It might be loud. Don't be scared."

"It's ok. I'm not afraid."

"Good."

Elijah sauntered onto the testing platform, sunlight once more stabbing him in the eyes. He squinted. Peter was standing at the rail. It was a straight shot from Elijah's mark to Peter's head. Elijah noted the sharp angle before shouting the countdown into the microphone. "Commencing test in 3...2...1!"

Ignition started. The flame burned beneath the tanks, heat radiating against his legs. The thrust felt balanced on his back.

*Fuel intake steady. Good start.* He started to rise. A foot from the ground, then three, then five. He rose to be eye-level with Peter.

"Good work, Elijah! Now, how does it maneuver?"

Elijah rose further and began to swoop around the dome like a bird on a wind gust, effortlessly turning, ducking, and rolling. Peter had asked for a machine that could move too quickly for anyone to target; Elijah, for the moment, gave him what he wanted.

Clapping hands rang in the domed testing pad. Peter was pleased. His microphone carried his voice: "Come here! I'll set you free now."

*There is no freedom for me,* Elijah thought. He kicked the throttle and rose higher. As he hovered above Peter, he verified the angle and started his shot. Like a guided bomb, he aimed for Peter's chest.

As Elijah veered toward him, Peter tried to get away, his feet skittering across the stone platform. The first few frantic backward steps tripped him up and splayed him across the platform.

*Better target.*

In his peripheral vision, Elijah saw Sancho climb the stairs and stand at the edge of the platform. *Always too late.* Elijah almost kissed Peter when he reached him, foreheads touching for a moment before the explosion.

Hot pressure knocked Sancho off his feet, almost sending him down the stairs. His back plastered to the wall, he called "Elijah!" but heard nothing. Called again. Nothing. Again, noticing now that he couldn't hear his own voice. He clapped his hands to his ears, as if trying to thump sound back into them. Nothing.

Sancho kept his hands to the ground, feeling along the stone for something, anything to tell him what happened. Slinking forward on hands and knees, he found bits of hot metal (which he promptly dropped), smelled burning fuel, and finally grasped a charred piece of flesh.

Tears fell as he grasped more burnt body parts. He called for Elijah, for Peter. Hearing nothing, Sancho was left only with the charred remains, unable to tell the difference between who had been kind to him and who had been cruel.

# FLIGHT TO MARS

## MATT SINCLAIR

The trip to Mars is delayed. If it isn't nerve-wracking enough that our flight faces a shrinking window before the planets spread much further – bumping up the price -- we risk the prospect of flying into a looming meteor shower if the trip is held up for days.

So, instead of worrying about what I can't control, I sit in a softly spinning grav-bar at the launch port sipping a lunar lager. You take the bad with the good.

I don't know why I agreed to start a franchise of my cousin's coffee company. I was happy with my job as the chief executive for North American coffee sales, and it has been years since I ran a franchise.

But this one is unique. It's more than just a franchise. Ours will be the first coffee company on Mars.

Say what you will, but starting a new business venture on another planet has more challenges than advantages. Innovating agro-technologies, establishing new relationships, learning how the culture is different. Mars may be an Earth colony, but people have been living there for years now. They're humans, but they're Martians.

Still, my cousin is right about it being a terrific opportunity. I've made a bundle of money before ever setting foot on the planet. The advertising opportunities blossomed before I hired any staff. That was nice, and I was able to hire an HR executive to staff the other people we need.

Money has been rolling in and we haven't even entered full negotiations with any of the colonies. Plus, it's not as though we can grow coffee beans there yet.

I am looking forward to the trip to Mars. The adventure of visiting the colonies is exciting, but it also means old-fashioned face-to-face meetings. Although the tech has improved since the Mars colony was established in 2076, it still takes forever to conduct a meeting via holo-conference. And while traditional email is more efficient, it takes a long time for the data to travel those millions of miles.

Granted, we're still setting things up with the colonial government, and I haven't started negotiations with the municipal governments. One of the first things transplanted to Mars was bureaucracy.

Nearly twenty years after the first colony was established on Mars, we're at least another year away from breaking soil on the first Martian coffee farm. At least. If the first crop is in place before the turn of the century, I'll be a happy Earther.

As I sit waiting to hear about the status of my flight, I meet my first Martian. She's tall. I'd read about how the difference in gravity causes those born on Mars to be long and lean, but I didn't quite fathom what it meant.

Standing at least seven feet tall, she catches the bartender's attention.

"Martian Red Ale," she says.

It's the same as the Earthling red ales since there aren't any breweries on Mars either (which I know because I've begun discussions with the colonial government about that venture, too.)

She is holding out her paper money.

"Forty," says the bartender, as he hands her the drink.

"But the price is listed as seventeen," she replies. Though her voice displays little emotion, her eyes narrow.

"That's in Lunar Lira," the bartender replies. "In your Martian money, it's forty."

Eying an opportunity, I negotiate a deal. "Put it on my tab," I say. "This way I can honestly tell my boss I've completed my first deal with a Martian on my trip."

"Thank you," she says. We clink our glasses and each take a sip.

"I'm Tom," I say.

She shakes the hand I offer. Her grip is soft, as though she isn't quite sure what to do with it. Her hand feels delicate. Fragile, like she has the bones of a bird.

She replies at the same time something crashes behind the bar, but I think I catch her name. "I have a sister named Laura," I say.

"No, Lura. Spelled like 'Luna' but with an 'r'."

I smile. That's actually a well-known name on Mars, according to my research. "You're the first Lura I've met."

She looks at her glass. I can't tell if she is embarrassed, ashamed, or perhaps just thinking about the beer.

"You're also the first Martian I've met," I continue.

"I'm not surprised. I'm often the first Martian Earthers meet. Some call me the first Martian." She sipped her beer again and seemed unimpressed with the flavor.

"How do you mean?"

"I was the first child born there," she says.

Did I gasp? "You're *that* Lura?" For an interplanetary celebrity, she seems so calm and unassuming.

She sips her beer.

"I haven't been to Earth since I was a young child," she continues. And that was the only time. My grandmother died. I had only known her through video and holo-calls. But I was very sad."

"I'm sorry."

A garbled announcement comes over the loudspeaker, followed almost immediately by a message on my wrist. I see Lura pull an old phone from a vest pocket I hadn't noticed.

"If we're lucky, we can beat the meteor shower," I say.

"Are we on the same flight?"

"If you're heading to Mars, then yes," I reply.

Her smile isn't broad, but it's there.

Lura grabs a small bag off the floor. It's like watching a heron touch its wing to the ground. Beautiful, yet awkward. A woman that tall should not carry such a small bag, much less leave it on the floor.

The way she struggles, I assume the bag is heavy.

I suck down the last of my beer. "Can I help you with your bag?"

"I'm fully capable of carrying my own bag," she chirps.

I probably go red in the face. "I didn't mean to sound boorish. I apologize."

She sighs. "It's all right, Tom. But Martians have different experiences with gravity. And a grav-bar is set to Earth standards."

"I wasn't thinking," I say. My head drops a little. "I guess Mars will be a bigger adjustment for me than I anticipated."

We walk to the terminal together. Once we're out of the grav-bar, the launch port's walkway system is a slight adjustment; it uses gravity levels closer to that of the moon than those of Earth, but enough that we can walk.

"Why are you traveling to Mars?" she asks, once we are in line for our ship.

My cousin had suggested I keep a low profile. I motion for her to lower her head, and I whisper to her, "I'm opening the first coffee franchise on the planet."

Her vacant look is not what I expect. "What is that?" she asks.

The robotic flight attendants ask for our flight information. "I'll tell you more inside," I say to Lura.

We run our wrists under the scanner, where our itineraries are registered. "Thomas Evers, sleep unit seven," the mechanical voice tells me.

Lura would be in unit three.

"I'm often in that one," she says as we head toward the ship. "They only have four sleep units for Martians."

"Why is that?"

She rolls her eyes. "To be fair, not many of us fly. Not even to the moon. But with my new responsibilities, I expect to visit the moon several times a year," she says. "Martian year," she clarifies. "That's closer to two Earth years."

The entrance to the ship has lunar levels of gravity. I've been to the moon several times now, but I still enjoy entering and exiting a shuttle. I bounce up the steps and grin as I enter the ship and watch Lura climb slowly toward the entrance. She bends to enter. Clearly, the ship is designed with Earthers in mind.

We find our sleep units. As indicated on the console, the departure time is scheduled for fifteen minutes. Enough time to prepare for going into stasis, but not much else.

Another Earther enters her unit between us, and Lura steps toward me. "Do we have time? I'd like to learn about coffee," she says softly.

For the next few minutes, I tell her about coffee and its history, how Earthers use it to give them a jolt of energy in the morning and have done so for centuries. Lura was unfamiliar with tea as well, and I share some of its history.

An announcement relays throughout the cabin, informing us that all passengers must enter their stasis chambers. "A shame," I say. "I would have enjoyed talking with you about coffee and learning about your world."

"We must meet on the planet. We'll make arrangements when we arrive."

We shake hands again, and though her handshake still feels delicate, her smile seems warm, strong, and genuine.

The trip to Mars is uneventful, by design. By going into stasis for the trip, which takes a few weeks of earth time with the latest generation of ion-powered travel, we are completely incapacitated. Not so much as a dream passes through my brain. Back on Earth, philosophers and scientists debate whether we actually age during these trips, but it seems like the wrong argument to me; what is lost by not experiencing and thinking through the trip itself? Perhaps nothing, but I'm curious to find out.

True to her word, Lura and I make plans after our arrival on Mars for the following sol.

All the people I meet are from Earth, so they already know — and miss — coffee. "What did they say a century ago?" one of the government officials commented, "There's a Starbucks on every corner? I wonder how long it'll take until that type of ubiquity comes to Mars."

My meetings go well, but I had no idea how tired I would be afterward. I could really use a cup of coffee; the caffeine pills don't quite cut it.

I finish the sol's meetings enthusiastic about our prospects and looking forward to what seems like a fait accompli. But the excitement I feel in seeing Lura is like a shot of espresso.

Given the lack of coffeeshops and bars on the planet, we meet at her office. Lura has an interesting career. Though she works as a scientist, researching various soils of Earth and its revivified moon and studying how to improve the arability of her home planet, she also serves in the parliament of her region and is running for the Martian Congress.

"I'm amazed at how much you all do here on Mars," I tell her. "You're involved in so many different things."

"We are a colonial world," she explains. "There simply is too much work to be done and not enough people. It is as it must be."

"That's why you need coffee," I say. I mean it to be funny, but she looks concerned.

"Actually, Tom, I fear that is why you will have difficulty selling your coffee."

After what I had heard earlier, I am a bit surprised.

"But the people I spoke with were so encouraging."

She nods. "That's because they're Earthers. I don't know if Martians have need of such products." She offers her Mona Lisa smile. "I hope I am wrong about that."

I shift in the chair and look out the window at the rust-colored world. Before I'd left for Mars, my cousin had commented that selling coffee to Martians might not be a slam-dunk. "There are no guarantees," he said. "Just do your best. We still have half the Lunar market, but Mars is worth the risk."

I turn back to Lura. "How big is the Martian population?"

She leans against her chair. "I suspect you do not realize, but that could be considered an offensive question among my people," she says. "I like you, Tom. You honestly believe you have something the people of Mars want. And you may even be correct."

"How did I offend you?"

She smiles. "You did not. But on Mars there is a difference between the 'Martian population' and the population of Mars. If you lived here, you would be an Earther on Mars, not a Martian."

I consider her words. "How many people live on Mars, and how many of them are native Martians?"

She nods. "Those of us born on Mars number approximately a hundred thousand. We are a small minority on a planet of some five million. But we are growing more significant every day."

The calculations aren't hard; there's a sizeable coffee market.

"And I suspect most of us have never heard of coffee, and even fewer have drunk it."

I know he won't see it right away, but I send my cousin an urgent email the next sol.

*Change in plan. In addition to coffee, I'm working on a way to include a drink called 'Qater' on our menu. It's a Martian beverage that appeals to natives who've never had coffee. Also working on partnership with local government official to introduce Qater to Moon and Earth.*

The new meetings I schedule add a week to my itinerary, but with my cousin's blessing we corner both the coffee market and establish an interplanetary Qater market.

Lura and I coordinate our schedules to travel to the Moon together.

Before our departure, we meet at a small restaurant at the launch port.

She is smiling when I arrive.

"You had a successful trip, it seems," she says as we shake hands.

"Far better than I expected. And I owe so much of it to you."

"We shall see," she replies. "You have much work to do before you return to Mars."

I smile broadly. "Indeed, I do. But the people you have put me in touch with could become famous on an interplanetary level. Their recipe for Qater will become the standard for people on Earth. And we've already begun promoting the arrival of the product. I suspect you'll be meeting with additional Earthers to enter your markets."

She nods. "We shall see."

For several months after the beginning of the Martian Revolution, our coffee shops on Earth become targets for violence and protest. Needless to say, once the Martians, led by Lura's party, come into power and declare independence of Earth, Qatar becomes a huge loser on our menu, and coffee on Mars is still too expensive to be viable. At this point, my stores sell nothing but Qater and warm beer.

I'm still able to travel to Mars, but every business trip is scrutinized by both governments, and most of my communication with the franchises is done via email. It's been that way for the past four Earth years. But in the wake of the second election after Martian independence, I schedule a trip to meet with the new government.

The invitation to the office of the Martian Prime Minister is a surprise, however. Of course, I know Lura has been elected to the post, but relations between the two planets have deteriorated so badly that we lost half the franchise locations we'd had at the end of our first year on Mars. Earth year.

But you might say the company has a monopoly. No other Earth companies have a presence on Mars. I'm not talking simply beverages. No other companies. To some on Earth, my company is traitorous. At my cousin's direction, I base my operations on the moon, but I have to visit the Mars headquarters from time to time.

Outside her office, Lura's assistant tells me I have ten minutes with the Prime Minister. Frankly, that seems like a long time, and I wonder what Lura has in mind.

"Tom!" she says as I am brought into her office.

"Madame Prime Minister." The aide closes the door quietly behind me.

"Oh, stop," she says, her smile beaming. "Lura, please." She directs me to an Earther chair that doesn't quite go with the décor, as if it had been brought in for the meeting, she continues. "*You* may call me Lura."

Her chair is larger, befitting her Martian frame. "Neither of us would be in the positions we are in if not for the other," she says.

She has become quite adept at politics, I realize. "You're quite right," I reply.

I look around the pyramid-shaped office. It is spartan, with just her desk, a few chairs surrounding a small table (I know not to call it a coffee table), and an old-fashioned computer console. Through the single window, I see the distant sun setting over the rust-colored planet. The same sun I have always known.

"Thank you, Lura. But I was not expecting this gracious invitation, much less the amount of time you are providing."

She smiles. "You have always been perceptive," she says. "And *receptive*. You recognize opportunities, Tom, and that's what I hope I have for you."

"And for you, I presume."

"The best opportunities are always of mutual benefit."

I look around the office again and find myself uncomfortable in the silence. There is no hum of conversation or background noise. The room holds but just ourselves.

"If I may be so bold, Lura, I suspect whatever you're going to suggest also has mutual danger."

She sits back in her chair and stretches a long leg over the other. Our eyes catch each other. The room is so silent, I hear the wind outside the tightly sealed windows.

"Perhaps more perceptive than I remember," she says.

She gazes at the ceiling. "My chief of staff cautioned me that the risks were not worth the reward." She straightens herself in her chair. "But that is why he is chief of staff and I am Prime Minister."

My stomach tightens and for the first time I recognize the power of the Martian Prime Minister.

"Let me assure you," she resumes, and in what seems a casual manner she relaxes her legs once more, resting her elbows on her knees, and leans toward me. "You can say no to what I'm about to suggest. It will not affect your ability to sell your products as you do now or in the future. At least as long as I'm in office. Frankly, I don't want anything to appear different at all."

My mouth is dry and my voice cracks slightly. "There seems to be a 'but' in there."

"Not intentionally. If you succeed in what I'm going to suggest, you may usher in a new age of cooperation between our planets. All we want is mutual respect."

The silence returns.

"And if I fail?"

Lura lightly taps my knee. Like the rest of my body, my legs go numb. "Honestly, Tom, that's harder to predict."

She stands, and by protocol I know I should stand, too, but I'm not sure my legs can work. She hasn't made a proposal yet, and my blood seems to have stopped flowing.

She walks to her desk and pulls two bottles of beer from underneath. Not a brand I sell.

And it's cold.

She pops them open and I see the condensation rise on the bottles.

"Lura, where did you get those?"

She smiles and walks toward me. "Is that really your question?" She hands me a cold beer and raises hers to mine.

I stand.

"Taste," she says.

We sip our beers.

"You have cold beer on Mars, Lura! How?"

She takes another sip and offers a pleased sigh. "The challenge," she says, "is to keep these on ice."

"Ice is prohibitively expensive here," I say.

"Yes. But more importantly, we do not have basic refrigeration technology on the planet. It is prohibited to ship Earth refrigeration technology to Mars."

I am confused. I've always had access to the technology. It's too expensive to run the electricity on Mars, which is why my stores don't do it, but refrigeration had been around since the twentieth century, and even before then Earthers used ice from lakes to keep things cool.

"What made Mars habitable was the ability to generate water on planet," I say. "Why can't you generate ice? You know how cold it is on the surface."

"It is not merely about refrigeration. It is also filtration," she says. "The sharing of such technology is prohibited, even though on Earth it would qualify as public domain information. Martians must develop this technology on planet."

Lura sits and rests her elbows on her knees once more. "The embargoes between our planets, which are many decades old, do not allow shipments of the materials needed to build such facilities at the scale we require."

I take another sip of beer. "Doesn't that give you the opportunity to develop new partnerships with Earth?

She shakes her head. "Political suicide. At least in the short term. As the first democratically elected Prime Minister since the revolution, I need to focus on the challenge of building independence and stability on Mars."

I stand and walk to the window. I enjoy another sip of beer.

"Are most Martians familiar with cold beer?"

She smirks. "Those who try it on the Moon like it very much."

"But it's crazy expensive there," I offer, "because your money is still undervalued."

The Prime Minister rises and walks toward me; it is Lura, however, who elbows me.

"Unless, of course, a kind, curious Earther is willing to buy a girl a drink. With his money." She raises her glass and we clink them together again.

As far as I am aware, my cousin has no clue I have been smuggling materials from our lunar facilities; I bribe the Martian customs officers with Earth cash. And Lura's office quashes the various local interest stories that include references to cold beer that pop up on occasion.

She assumes that Earth agencies are following the Martian sites to pick up on potential insurrections and developments that have propaganda value. I don't know whether she's right, but I appreciate that she has thought of it.

But when my secretary hands me tickets to Earth, I have a feeling it isn't simply about the scheduled board of directors meeting.

My cousin's secretary, a young Martian named eLesa, who I had helped place soon after I launched our Martian businesses, smiles when I arrived. "Mr. Evers asked me to tell you he needs a few more minutes," she says, "but you're welcome to wait here in the lobby."

I know my cousin and most of his peers call her "Lisa" since the initial 'E' is more a breath than a pronounceable sound. But I thank her using her Martian pronunciation.

"Have you eaten?" she asks. "If you like, I can have some refreshments sent here."

"That's ok. I'm just going to get a little exercise after the flight," I tell her. "I'll buy something in the cafeteria. I haven't had a burger in months."

"I'll send a page to your wrist when it's time," eLesa replies.

It takes a little longer than usual for my credits to be acknowledged when I buy lunch. And I notice several people peering my way. I sense an element of disgust with my presence. It wasn't that long ago I was seen as the lucky son of a gun who'd cornered the Martian market and made the company a ton of money. I was the connection to Mars, but the vibe I was getting from Earthers in the cafeteria is uncomfortable.

The intercom system crackles. "Thomas Evers, please report to the board room," drones a mechanical voice.

I haven't heard such an announcement my entire career; we have wrist communication for a reason.

As I look at my wrist, a message arrives from eLesa.

*Lura says report to flight deck 4 immediately.*

Lura?

An executive secretary of an Earth company does not refer to the Prime Minister of another planet, not even her home planet, by her first name.

Trouble is brewing. I have to tread carefully.

I toss my remaining meal away and head to the hall. I feel the eyes in the cafeteria following me.

Once I am out of the room, I receive another message. It's a diplomatic visa for a Lunar cargo flight. Flight Deck 4.

I pass a few people who barely acknowledge my presence and others who glare at me. Despite my racing heart, I walk. Although the flight decks are on the same level as the corporate suites, I don't trust the elevator. It might send me to the corporate suite, because that is where the system has me going. But what if someone stops me on the rarely used stairs? I think about how I'd answer any question I'm asked and am relieved to reach the flight deck, where the door is held open by a young male Martian. He says nothing as I step onto the ship without a word.

The intercom pages me again. This time my cousin's voice calls for me. "Tommy, where are you?"

The door to the ship closes. I find a seat and prepare for take-off. It's a Martian seat, and I feel small.

The same Martian who let me in sits beside me. "Myrek,' he says and offers his hand. His thin smile worries me, but I shake his hand. "If you like, I can serve you some coffee from my home planet."

I chuckle nervously. "My coffee isn't sold on Mars anymore."

"That's true. But the Prime Minister's office has a regular supplier."

My jaw must have dropped.

"I believe you're familiar with the provider."

Of course I am; it's me.

During the trip to the moon, Earth Global reports me as a fugitive, though the news indicates that I'm still on the planet. My picture appears on screens throughout the ship; it's a cargo transport: destination Luna. At least that's what the manifest I pull up indicates.

Myrek, who had left the small passenger area once we were out of Earth orbit, returns. My legs twitch as fast as my heart beats. Our earlier conversation suggested not only that he knows who I am but that he works for the Martian government. I rap my fingers repeatedly against the arm rest.

"Slight change in plans," he says. I must have blanched. "We will need to slingshot around the moon and head directly to Mars. No lunar landing."

My mouth goes dry. "We anticipated this possibility. Shifting flight plans might alert Earth to your presence, however."

"Do we have enough fuel?" I ask. My voice crackles.

He nods. "That's the good news. The bad news is since we're a cargo ship, we have limited use of ion power."

"So it'll take much longer to get there than usual."

Myrek kneels slowly; the gravity boots make it difficult for anyone, but it looks especially awkward for a Martian. "That's part of it. There's also a possibility that Earth or your company will send a ship to intercept us before we reach Mars."

I look at the ceiling.

"And Martian cargo transports do not use sleep inducers, so we have an exciting trek through mostly empty space."

"Mostly empty?"

"Our shields are strong enough to repel at least 98 percent of meteorites."

I curse under my breath. The company has lost two ships to meteorite damage over the past three Earth years. "I suppose it's better than being tried as a smuggler."

"Or worse," Myrek says.

"Worse?"

"The latest news is branding you a planetary traitor."

"I can't go home?"

"Not as a free man."

My head reels. "Will I be welcome on Mars?"

Some Martians have very odd laughter. A low, guttural sound, it makes me think of an alligator trilling. Myrek's makes me think of dinosaurs. "What's so funny?" I ask.

"You're the first Earther welcome on Mars since the revolution," he says. "I expect you'll be meeting with the Prime Minister once you're back on the planet. With her in your corner, you're more than welcome."

✡

Over the quiet months of travel, Myrek teaches me several Martian card games, which are difficult in zero-G. They are variations of Earth games, of course, since all the earliest people on Mars were Earther colonists.

Assuming Earth can intercept our messages, he sends nothing beyond the usual, and we receive no word of any Earth ships heading to Mars. Still, each time I look out the window at the black emptiness, I expect to see an approaching ship.

A space voyage at sub-ion speed, frankly, is boring. Neither Myrek nor I have much room to exercise, much less any equipment, and the lack of gravity seems to cause me to waste away. Myrek's gravity boots don't fit my feet, so I spend much of my time literally up in the air.

With so much time, it's impossible not to worry about the future. I have nothing. No home. No family. It doesn't feel like they have died; it feels like I have. Will anyone on Earth care that I'm gone?

When we land, I am removed from the ship on a medical floatation stretcher and spend another few days in a government hospital to readapt to gravity and regain muscle mass. While I recuperate, I enjoy my first glass of Martian ice water.

As Myrek predicted, I am brought to the Prime Minister's office after my release from the hospital. I walk in using a cane. This time, we are not alone. Two deputy ministers shake my fragile hands and tell me how honored they are to meet me.

"We didn't bring you here simply to say thank you, however, Tom," Lura says.

I turn around, worried that I might see someone from the company emerge through another door. Or worse, a team of police intent on removing me from the planet. "What's going on?"

Lura returns to her desk and picks up a device I don't recognize. It reminds me of an ancient handgun.

"We would prefer that you not be deemed a political dissident," says one of the deputy ministers.

Lura inserts something into the device and softly grabs my arm. "You have been granted Martian citizenship," she says. And she injects a new chip into my forearm beside my Earther chip. "You also have been granted the first license to make, sell, and distribute coffee on the planet since the revolution."

I lean against my cane afraid I might collapse. A wave of relief washes through my body. I am an Earther-Martian. I might not be able to leave my adopted planet, but I have a place to call home.

"Turns out you were right," she adds with a smile. "After you start drinking that stuff, it's hard to start your day without it."

"It's pleasant over ice, too," I reply.

# THE SWEET YET BITTER

## KATHRYN ROSSATI

The hessian sack over Parro's head was clean, not dust-ridden and mildew-stained as she had expected. Then again, the soldiers guiding her and the rest of the group of potential royal poisoners were members of the King's personal guard. They wouldn't dare inflict more discomfort than was necessary on someone who might end up in a position to have them permanently removed from their posts.

Under her soft boots, the evenness of the flagstones was a welcome change from the three miles of cobblestones they'd just walked. It also signaled to her that they were finally nearing the castle. Perhaps they were already in the courtyard.

As she was marched through a maze of sharp-turning corridors, she heard the guards bark at any servant who wasn't quick enough to scurry from their path. When they finally ordered the party to halt, a rush of air brushed her cheek in time with the groaning of a heavy door opening. Then once again she was guided forward with the others.

After a few steps, the door banged shut and Parro's sack was snatched from her head, allowing her a view of the King's private audience chamber. The room was windowless, the only light coming from bright torches burning in iron sconces on the walls. The floor was tiled with grey granite, and the room was covered in great tapestries and wall hangings Parro could only guess depicted the country's bloody history. The royal banner hung at the far end, above the filigreed silver throne in which the King sat ready. His manservant stood next to him, so still that he could be mistaken for a statue.

The King's attention was fixed on the poisoners, whose anxious whisperings surrounded Parro. She dismissed their distracting fuss and stole a glance at the monarch's face. His expression was flat and disciplined, but his eyes stared back at her with a keen intelligence. She quickly dropped her head. Curse her curiosity! It would not do to give herself away just yet, she couldn't afford any more mistakes.

The captain of the guard made the poisoners stand in line, facing the interior of the room, where a table adorned with various apparatuses was ready for the demonstrations that Parro assumed would soon take place. She caught sight of another group of people gathered in a dark corner. She focused her vision and saw that they were shackled together. Prisoners. At least that answered the question of just how the demonstrations were to be carried out.

"I presume they have all been checked, Captain?" the King said when the preparations had been completed.

"Of course, sire. I personally checked each candidate, only one of them had any marks pertaining to either spy or assassin guilds, and I dealt with him as soon as I found them," the captain replied, tapping the hilt of his sword meaningfully.

The King raised a bushy eyebrow. "Oh, from which guild?"

"The Oens, sire."

The King grunted. "The Oens? I'm surprised one of theirs made it as a candidate at all. It seems our selection protocol has become rather lax of late."

The captain stiffened. "I shall see to it that proper disciplinary action is taken, sire."

"Good. Now, I think we should proceed, don't you?"

The captain bowed and turned to address the poisoners. "I shall call you one at a time to present your skills. You may request as many prisoners to use for your demonstrations as you wish, but do not bore us with flowery words. Be direct, be swift, and be thorough. Once your demonstration is complete, you must return to your place in line and wait while the other candidates present their skills." He took a scroll from his belt pouch and unrolled it, reading out the first name on the list. "Lector Heeny, please present yourself to His Royal Majesty, King Theroux the Second, Ruler of all Mentrolis."

A thin, trembling man stepped into the center of the room, carrying a neat wooden chest in his skeletal hands. He set it on the table and opened it, taking out a myriad of vials and boxes, as well as a bottle of clean water, and began mixing various ingredients together with the implements that had been provided.

Parro stifled a yawn. The man's poisons were basic and the tremor in his hand as he called for his first prisoner betrayed the fact that he had not once stayed to watch his victims die.

The prisoner, a middle-aged woman whose threadbare pantaloons reeked of the fresh urine that stained them, struggled against the guards as they dragged her toward Lector Heeny. The poisoner gave a stammered speech to the King as to what the poison he had mixed would do, and then asked the guards to hold the woman's head so he could poor the miniscule measure of green liquid down her throat. The pitiful man could hardly bear to look at her as he instigated her death.

The woman choked and tried to cough it up, but already her muscles had begun to seize. Within seconds, her entire body became stiff and she fell to the cold floor. Lector Heeny shuddered and turned away, already mixing the next poison for his demonstration.

So it went on. Poisoner after poisoner was called to display their lackluster skills, while the bodies of their victims were hauled away and covered with a dark sheet. The King neither displayed his displeasure, nor acknowledged the candidates in any way... until Parro was called.

She walked to the table and swept the equipment laid out for her onto the floor in a single, smooth motion. "Excuse me, your Majesty," she said as they shattered, before putting her own bag on the tabletop.

The King raised one bushed eyebrow. "It is unusual for a woman to be in your line of profession," he remarked.

"I assure you that my skills are not lacking. In fact, to be worse than these other *candidates* would be impressive indeed, your Majesty," she said.

The King snorted in amusement. "I hope for your sake that your confidence is not unfounded."

Parro smiled and opened the clasp on her bag with a snap. From within, she pulled out two serving trays with domed metal covers, concealing the contents inside, and laid them on the table with a deft flourish of her arm.

"What is this, woman?" the captain snapped, rushing forward. "His Majesty has called for poisoners, not a serving wench. How dare you waste his—"

"Captain, stand down," the King said, holding up his hand. "Let her proceed."

The captain stepped back, his expression incredulous. "But sire—"

"Captain, if you disobey me, it will be *your* tongue on which this woman's poisons will fall. Is that clear?"

"Yes, sire," the captain replied, his face greying. He turned to Parro. "Proceed, woman."

"Why, thank you, Captain," she said. Parro took a bottle from her case and placed it next to the first serving tray. Then she addressed the King directly. "Your Majesty, there are a vast number of poisons in this world and, while effective, a great many of these now have known antidotes. Though these antidotes are only available for a substantial sum, they are not out of reach for those of a high societal standing. It has also become expected that when hosting a feast at court, someone is sure to be the target of a poisoner's deft hand, so people are being more cautious than ever. Even the ambassadors of Importa and Tlousin, whom I believe have recently lost your favor, have prepared themselves for such."

Surprise flickered across the King's face, but he regained his control quickly. "You have kept yourself well informed, woman. However, what is your point on this matter?"

"My point is simple, your Majesty. There is a growing need for new poisons, and I have concocted one that I believe you'll find most interesting."

Parro lifted the domed cover from the first tray as she spoke, revealing a curried dish boasting a hue of deep orange. The fine use of spices in the sauce made the dish so aromatic that it almost chased away the stench of the prisoners. Almost.

"That is *Umbren*, is it not? A staple served widely in Tlousin," the King remarked.

"And a favorite of Lord Enru, the ambassador of Tlousin," the captain added. "He demands we request ingredients for it all the time."

"Indeed," Parro said. "The first poison I wish to demonstrate only reacts with certain seasonings, which means that if administered in any other food or drink, it will be harmless. It also merges with the ingredients so well that it becomes untraceable; even a practiced healer examining the stomach contents of the victim would not find it."

She clicked her finger to the guards. "Two prisoners," she said. As the guards brought them to her, she undid the cork on the bottle, added several drops to the curried dish, and poured a measure onto a spoon, again taken from her bag. "Observe, your Majesty." Forcibly opening the first prisoner's mouth, she let the poison drip straight onto his tongue from the spoon. Then, taking a clean spoon, she took a level scoop of the curry and force-fed it to the second prisoner. Satisfied, she stepped aside so the King could see the effects in full.

While the first prisoner made a face of disgust, the second fell to the ground without so much as a cry.

"As you can see, with this poison, there is no violent frothing, convulsing, or bleeding. The man might have died naturally of a brain clot, for all anyone need know."

"I see you were not merely boasting after all," the King said.

Parro inclined her head, acknowledging the compliment, and turned to the second serving tray, again removing the dome to reveal the contents. On the tray was a glass gravy boat, but instead of holding brown liquid, it was filled with a condiment that gave off a distinctly tart yet honeyed aroma. "This is a popular new sauce for meats that has made its way here from the continent. I am sure your chefs are already perfecting the recipe. What they do not know, however, is that this sauce is a poison far more deadly than any you have seen today. The reason why no one realized this, including your chefs, is that by themselves, the ingredients are harmless. As with other spices and herbs, it is only when they are mixed that they become potent. They kill very, very slowly. Not only that, but the taste is believed to be so divine that the consumer quickly becomes addicted."

The King stood up abruptly. "Are you trying to tell me that someone from the continent is bold enough to poison *me*, woman?"

Parro walked around to the front of the table and faced the King directly. "That is exactly what I'm telling you, your Majesty."

"What makes you so convinced that my chefs are indeed planning to serve me this... relish?"

Parro's gaze moved to the King's manservant, whose statue-like demeanor diminished by the second. "If someone were to sample even a spoonful of this sauce, it would leave certain traces."

"Which are?" the King pressed.

"A distinct greening of the cuticles and yellowing of the eyes," she replied.

The King turned to his manservant, whose hands were shaking as he examined his fingers, seeing that Parro was correct. "Will I... will I die?" the manservant asked.

"Yes, unless you take the antidote. Fortunately, I have it with me, but I need to examine you and the kitchen staff thoroughly to determine the dosage."

"Of course, lady, I—"

"No," the King said. "If my staff were foolish enough not to realize what this relish truly is, then their fate is of their own doing. I see no reason to save anyone so careless."

Parro pursed her lips. "Careless? What an interesting thing to say, your Majesty."

The King stared back at her, his eyes cold. "Woman, from the moment I first laid eyes on you, I have felt that you have been hiding something. At first, I was intrigued, but now you are testing my patience."

"Your Majesty, I am but a humble poisoner. My standing is so lowly that in your eyes I am sure it must feel as though I am from a completely *different world*. However, *I* have nothing to hide."

The King's face turned ashen at her words. He turned swiftly and pressed a jewel on the arm of his throne. A section of the back wall shifted forward and then to the side with a loud grinding. In its place was a slight opening. "Guards, remain here. Woman, follow me," he snapped, and disappeared through the gap. Parro followed.

After walking through a short tunnel, they entered a small, square room adorned with a simple desk, a chair, and a thin bookcase. As soon as Parro passed the threshold, the King shut the door. "Who are you?"

In reply, Parro took a small pot of balm from her belt pouch and, rolling up her long sleeve, spread a thin layer onto the pale skin of her left arm. Instantly, iridescent numbers appeared on the surface.

"An android," the King sniffed. "I should have known. From the agency, I presume?"

"Yes, and so far, they've tracked you across three different dimensions. You've interfered with the development of every race you've encountered, and now you are posing as King. What did you do with the real one? Erase his memories and copy his form before deserting him in yet another dimension?"

To her surprise, he smirked. "Not a bad guess, android. Tell me, why are you here? I can't believe the agency would have you go through this charade just to arrest me."

"You were about to be poisoned by a concoction jointly developed by three different countries on the continent, and as you're the foremost expert on dimensional shift technology, the agency thought it unwise to let them proceed, tempting as it was. Proving myself as a candidate was the easiest way to gain your attention, with minimal disruption to this world."

"The poisoned sauce was real, then?"

"Yes, and soon I will have to give the antidote to your man-servant and your kitchen staff, as well as revive the prisoners your silly poisoners supposedly killed," Parro said curtly.

"Supposedly? I watched as life left them. There is no antidote for death."

"No, you only thought you saw them die because that's what you were expecting," Parro said. "Before we were all marched here, I drugged everyone and substituted their ingredients for ones that would give the expected reaction but not be lethal. Now, I must send a message to the agency informing them that the first part of my mission is complete."

"There's more to your orders?" the King asked.

She nodded. "I have to make sure that you restore the real king to his throne, as smoothly as possible. Make no mistake, though, your actions won't go unpunished."

"Oh, I do love your confidence. But the agency gave you in-complete information. I'm not just an expert on dimensional shift technology. I *invented* it. And you want to know the secret of how I've been doing it without access to the agency's shifting formula? Here," he said.

Without giving her time to react, he whipped a dagger from the inside of his robes and plunged it into her heart. A surge shot through her body as he removed the blade and watched her crumple to the ground.

Warnings of imminent shut down fired through her brain. What was happening? She couldn't be dying. The mission had to be a success. The agency depended on it.

In her fading vision as the connections in her body became systematically disabled, she caught an energy gauge on the dagger's hilt and saw the familiar symbol of the agency's winged crest flash on it.

"The energy from a dying being, even an android, is enough to fill my device to capacity," the King continued, kicking away her hand as she stretched feebly to take the dagger from his grasp. "I'll be sure to send word to the agency saying you played your part beautifully. Now, however, I must bid you farewell."

As the last part of her consciousness fought to remain, he pressed the jewel on the dagger's hilt and made a series of cuts in the air. The room blurred as he fled the dimension, leaving her body lying in a pool of silver blood.

# PRIMARY SEASON – LOVE RED ON PLANET BLUE

## JON FRIED

In the mid-Atlantic state of _____, thick southern air oppressed every unconditioned breath, and the people at opposing political rallies were wishing they were either by a pool, on a porch, or—more than anything—indoors. Or they were too pumped up on candidate spit, slogans, and home-team fervor to notice their own sweat; they were the lucky ones.

In the parking lot of the Rainbow School, a 23-year-old female Democrat in a full-body chicken suit was stomping back and forth in the space between the crowd melting on the asphalt and the portable stage, where a long-haired ninth-grade boy strummed a guitar and sang twelve verses of a song he'd written called, "Give Me My Planet Back," which he read off an iPad on a music stand. Each time he hit the chorus, she waved her wings and nodded her huge, orange-beaked head, silently urging the people to join. Many of them did, especially those in front, who might have been unconsciously afraid of the possibility that such a large version of a domesticated animal could suddenly become undomesticated, or who were feeling sorry for whoever it was trapped inside what had to be a very uncomfortable heat trap. They had no idea; Sarah was dying in there.

In the parking lot of the Columbus County Bank, a 32-year-old male Republican in a pink short-sleeved shirt, a pink tie, grey slacks, pig ears, a pig snout, and a pig tail attached to his belt roamed the crowd with a wireless mic making snorting sounds in every pause in the speech of an attractive blonde woman in her forties wearing a red dress and savaging both of the "Democrat" candidates vying for the opportunity to be trounced in November by the incumbent Republican governor, whom this loyal son of a GOP mucky muck had met a few times and couldn't stand. But he didn't mind his role today, which kept him on the move and allowed him to avoid chatting about the man, and he rather enjoyed the people in the crowd calling "soooooey" and clapping him on the shoulder as he passed, especially the girls in their stars-and-stripes tank tops. Boynton checked his watch. Might still be time for nine holes that afternoon. Only good thing about a day this hot was that not a soul at the club would be on the course.

Meanwhile, on a small, organic farm not too far away, a young actual chicken bemoaned her fate. Like the others, she'd arrived by mail (yes, by mail) as a fluffy little chick just a few weeks back. Like the others, she'd been kept under warm incubator lamps until she was old enough to run outside. Like the others, she found herself bunched by the door to the coop every morning, ready to scurry in a curving mass toward the food trough, which, when they found it empty, they would bypass and then run in another not-quite straight line *en masse* to the watering dish, which, when they found it empty, they would bypass and head toward their shade covering, where they huddled until they heard the food being poured into the trough. And then they would run back there.

Unlike the others, she was not, at six weeks, nine to eleven inches tall as promised in the catalog. She was almost twice that. And unlike the others, she was painfully aware of what was going on around her. She'd noticed with horror that some of the chicks packed in the mailing crate had not made it alive. She saw how the survivors spent their days, clucking and pacing aimlessly, sometimes scratching in the grass for bugs and seeds as their ancestors did, though they didn't really know how or why anymore. She understood that generations of breeding had left them useless for anything but a fate she guessed at and tried not to think about. By late in the day, many were lying down, tired after a big day of nothing, and by dusk most wandered back into the coop, though some had to be grabbed and tossed in (earlier in the day they would have clucked and flapped their non-flying wings in resistance, but not now). The only break in the routine came when a big bird flew overhead and, out of uncomprehending instinct, they ran for cover, either in higher grass, under the shade covering, or in the coop. The shade covering was moved every couple of days, and the first morning it was in a new place they still went to the old place because they had a memory of it and were too dumb to realize that there was no shade there anymore. Eventually some of them stumbled on to the new shade area and the rest followed.

This big hen, who looked down on the others physically but felt too much shame and sorrow at the fate she shared with them (and alone was conscious of) to look down on them as inferiors, nonetheless felt desperately alone, especially during the long hot days. She tended to wander to the edge of their grassy square and gaze across a gravel lot where cars and trucks came and went, past a dirt road and into a scrubby set of trees where she could see signs of another life, some large, unfamiliar creatures near the roots of those trees, and set her fading hopes in that direction.

As soon as the rally was over, Sarah wriggled out of the chicken suit, got in her car, and rushed over to the Slurp-Mart, a former 7-11 gone independent. She didn't care if the food colorings and sweeteners were awful for her, she'd earned it, and even if she hadn't earned, she wanted it. There was no boyfriend anymore, no Larry lecturing her all the time on the evils of corporate food-for-profit. For four weeks they'd been done, and she was trying to drown out that voice. Maybe a 32-ounce SuperSlurp would help. And it would be fun! Was there anything wrong with that? Larry didn't believe in fun. He was a Bernie-or-die guy who hated Hillary so much that, even now, almost a year later, he was blaming her for everything. Sarah had felt the Bern, too, but followed the logic that only Hillary could win. Oh logic, poor, useless logic! She and Larry would argue and she tried to keep her head, and he wouldn't and he'd be furious—and still want her as soon as the lights were out. He'd grumble impatiently at her immaturity when she wanted to wait a bit for at least something of a better mood. She'd been drawn to his maturity; he was 27 and never mentioned his parents, as if he had none. She'd held back her tears when he broke it off, mad at herself for being hurt at all when she'd been thinking about ending it, too. *Don't think about it now. Just get a SuperSlurp and cool off. Just ENJOY IT! Why is nothing simple? EVER?*

As soon as the rally was over, Boynton rushed into the Slurp-Mart, thinking how much he'd rather have a beer than a bottle of water, reminding himself yet again that he would have to stay strong if he didn't want to end up like his father who took any excuse to start drinking at any hour of the day. As soon as Boynton hit the AC, he paused, letting the relief begin. He looked at his phone. Amazing. Three and a half hours with no frantic calls, texts, or emails from anyone, work or personal. You have to appreciate the little things in life. He'd buy three waters, one for now, two for the back nine. Hell, make it four; if he was on his game, he might get the front nine, too. And isn't that a nice slender sight over by the SuperSlurp machine...

There's plenty of food in the trough. That's not why the pigs push and shove and snout-punch their way forward—and sometimes take a running start and launch themselves from the rear in an attempt to force their way to the front-and-center spot. They're just fighting to get one rung up the pig ladder, to win themselves some pointless, snort-grunting, pigs-only bragging rights.

The smallest pig of the litter stood back and shook his head in disgust. Twenty feet from the battleground was another trough also filled with food. They ignored it, no contest there. Food is not the point. He could have easily gone over to the second trough and if he gobbled quickly, gotten something of a meal before one of the other pigs noticed and ran over to shove him aside. The whole awful scene took his appetite away.

We pigs, so happy to fight over nothing! Taking our tiny pleasures where we can, scratching our sides against tree trunks, rolling and rooting in the mud, even if that mud is fouled with our own excrement—and blaming the filth on the ones below us on the pig ladder. We know better, too; we're not stupid. Bored out of our minds, we're still curious, following around the young man who comes with the food or tends to the electric fence we know not to bother with. This is the same young man who shows up now and then with a piece of plywood with handles on it and pushes one of us toward the ramp in back of the pickup truck that he's backed up into the sty. The unlucky one may evade his fate for a while, but as the truck pulls out, he's snorting away, telling the rest of us that he's got some tasty snacks, better than what we've got, and it doesn't look too bad from up there, and ha ha he's got it over us now, even though we all know he's never coming back and wouldn't want to be in his hooves right now. He knows it, too, but the momentary feeling of victory and superiority is stronger. They call this living? The little pig snorted and kicked the mud

He turned away from the feeding fracas. He wandered over to the electric fence. How hard would it be to burst through those two skinny wires? Not hard at all. A little sizzle on the skin. He'd felt it, he'd been curious, they all had. It wasn't the fence that kept them in the sty. It was the stupid, empty game they played.

As disgust gave way to despair, he gazed past the fence, across the road, across a gravel field beyond and saw a strange sight, what appeared to be a bird, larger than any bird he'd ever seen on the ground. And although the image was not very clear, he was fairly sure the bird – it could even be a chicken – was looking back at him. His heart lifted.

Sarah was mesmerized, nearly paralyzed, by the rainbow of shocking SuperSlurp choices before her, when she heard a deep, rich southern male's voice say, "Still got your leggings on."

She glanced at the polyester clinging to her otherwise bare legs—oh dear—and blushed—at the voice as much as the bright yellow—and then she looked over: a big, doughy, handsome caricature of every GOP stereotype that had ever kept her up at night, with a little pug nose and little blue eyes, but the decent manners to be turned half away so as not to admit he'd been looking her up and down and enjoying the utter distraction she'd created in his mind as he approached her at the SuperSlurp machine.

"Oh," she said and might have never said another word if she hadn't noticed what remained of his costume: the belt with the pink rubber corkscrew in the back. "You've still got your tail on."

He reached back quickly to confirm and then started to laugh, at himself and at the way a girl with a beak-like nose in a narrow face could not only be pretty but ravishingly so. And it wasn't just the big green eyes.

In a few minutes they established that each had been at the enemy's rally in similar roles and that only severe dehydration could explain how they would end up at the Slurp-Mart chatting so pleasantly. She glanced down and thought, *At least they make my legs look skinny*, while he was thinking, *Well they sure make her legs look nice.*

He admitted that without the belt his pants would fall down. "That's what you get for being thirty pounds overweight and then sweating off five pounds of water." And then he thought, *Why did I just say that?*

She admitted that she'd left on the leggings because she'd forgotten to wear shorts underneath. And she thought, *Why did I just say that?*

There was no doubt about why she'd been wearing the chicken costume: The urban blue part of the state called the man in the state house Governor Chicken because for months he'd been finding excuses to avoid press conferences so he wouldn't have to answer accusations of some collusion between government and industry that hadn't even occurred to him could be illegal until he saw some newscaster reading out the statute on TV. "So what's with the pig suit?" she asked, with a fearlessness she felt with almost no one, and which she could not entirely attribute to four hours in the sun covered in plastic and polyester.

"You know, I'm not even sure," he said, laughing again. He usually laughed easily, but not this easily. "Maybe law and order. Maybe hoping a boom economy will fatten up the place. Maybe because the governor comes from a long line of pig farmers. All I gotta say is thank God the elephant head was taken and they didn't make me dress up in some Boston Tea Party Indian regalia. I'm not one of those tea party nuts."

"What kind of nut are you?" she asked, surprising herself once again.

"My own, I guess."

She smiled. Even in the super-cool of the store, he still had a few drops of sweat on his upper lip. "How could you like that pig of a governor? Or chicken? Or whatever the hell he is?"

"I don't."

"Well good. And don't mention the president's name or I won't be able to speak to you."

"Fair enough."

She picked a color—purple—and he pulled some plastic water bottles from the big case and their conversation eased into non-partisan commentary about the primaries next Tuesday and the general in November, and he was just starting to tease her about using the word "gubernatorial," which always made him think of peanuts, when they heard what sounded like a gunshot followed by several screams and shouting and people fleeing and Boynton dropped his bottles and pulled Sarah to the floor.

If they'd had the chance to talk about it later, they each would have sworn that the other made the first step, that the inspiration was not their own. In fact, Big Hen and Little Pig make their moves at almost the same instant, Big Hen summoning whatever flight her wings would allow, Little Pig bursting between the wires and hardly feeling the 12-volt sting.

In moments they were in the road, eye to eye.

"We have to flee," he said.

She cocked her head quizzically, not understanding the snorts he'd uttered, but when he tossed his head back toward the woods, she understood, and they made their way.

They entered the trees not far from the pig sty, but none of the pigs noticed, lost as they were in their battle of pig egos and the search for passing pleasures.

The chickens had no idea she'd left, then or later.

"What..." Sarah was unable to finish her sentence.

"It's a hold up," he whispered.

Her SuperSlurp had fallen and burst open, and as purple goo spread across the white linoleum floor, she had the horrible fear that it was her blood and she'd been shot, even though there'd just been one bullet fired and it had gone into the ceiling. His hand on her shoulder calmed her enough so she could whisper, "It's the middle of a Saturday afternoon!"

"They're not always so bright," he said and then inched forward to peer beyond the aisle. As soon as he did, he lurched backward and said in a voice full of fear, "Oh shit, it's two white girls." He wriggled backward until he was cowering in a ball behind her.

"What..." she said again, even less able to finish her sentence.

In a trembling whisper he said, "Two black guys and I figure they just want money. Two white girls and I don't what the hell they're going to do."

Still quaking, Sarah nonetheless found herself thrilled at the thought of two fearless white girls and at the thought of Boynton's racism unmasked. And then a moment later she was ashamed of herself. Concentrate on safety!

Another gunshot and they both pressed their faces to the cold linoleum. Then with a squeal of tires from the parking lot it was over.

They eventually stood; Boynton recovered his cool, Sarah her voice. The cops came, they gave their statements and contact info, and were standing out in the lot between their cars, parked a few spots apart.

"I don't think I can drive," she said.

"I can wait with you."

"I gotta get out of here."

"OK," he said, and taking her arm, led her to his car, where he helped her in the passenger seat and once he'd started the engine and cranked the AC he turned to her and said, "I can take you home or I can buy you a drink. I know I could sure use one."

She'd never liked that phrase, 'I could use a drink.' Use to what end? Almost certainly not a good one.

"OK."

They found something of a path that led into the darkest woods. Her heart pounding, she began clucking away, hardly aware she was talking aloud. He had no idea what she was saying, but he could hear the tone: complaint and critique, followed by relief and excitement. And defiance. Intelligent defiance. He snorted back what he hoped was the same and she seemed to understand that he understood.

He kept slowing down so they could walk side by side. Up close he could see the beautiful black pattern across her chest. He snuffled a gentle compliment.

She found herself wishing she didn't have such a good sense of smell, and told herself it was just his skin, a skin he was trying to shed. It was just the filthy world he was born into, a world that together, just maybe, they were going to find a way to escape. And then as it mixed with the cool smells of the forest, she found herself liking it.

As the beer and everything else went to their heads, they admitted what fools they'd felt like at their rallies. They talked about how desperate people are for simple answers. He told her his mother was a Christian who didn't like church and his father did like church but was no Christian. He, Boynton, was a bit of both—he didn't like church and he was no Christian. "You can't teach people to love," he said. "You just got to love them and hope they figure it out."

She stared at him a minute. Then she talked about her parents and how they used to take her to rallies, the only times they were ever really nice to each other, and as she described them, they finally just seemed like people, especially her father.

They talked about couples they knew that had broken up over Trump, without mentioning the name. Repeating her ex-boyfriend Larry (despite herself), she said it didn't have to be, that Bernie could have won, that he would've won the coasts and the rust belt, and it wasn't fair that he didn't get the chance.

"Well, that we agree on."

The waitress asked if they wanted some food and they both had no appetite, but he ordered some fries anyway and they gobbled them up.

They didn't talk about the hold up.

Shielding their eyes from the brightness in the parking lot, she said, "Thank you, Boynton."

"People call me Boy," he said.

She laughed, hoping it wasn't rude.

"Look, I know this is going to sound funny, but if we want to keep talking, I know the guy who owns the motel right here. He's a good friend. I know what it sounds like, but where can you go on a hot day to just sit and talk and not have to eat or drink something?" The few times he'd made this suggestion before it had sounded old school. With this one he was afraid it sounded shabby.

"Libraries are closed on Saturday here," she said. "Thanks to certain budget cuts."

He held up his hands, thrust out his pink chin and said. "May-a culpa," exaggerating his southern drawl.

Little Pig was telling her of the rumors he'd heard that if these disgusting pathetic creatures called pigs returned to the wild—which they were perfectly capable of doing at any time, as he'd just proved—they'd revert to being wild boars. They'd sprout hair and tusks. They'd forage and thrive. Regain their dignity. And while she didn't exactly understand him, the way he motioned at the ground made her think of the foraging she would need to do to survive wherever it was they were going, and she was ready, even eager, to try. She flapped her wings as she struggled to keep up with him, trying not to catch her feathers on the low-lying twigs and leaves of the forest understory.

As they approached an undeniably glorious climax in the heavy-curtained, near darkness of the motel room, the part of her brain that could still think was chasing away the feeling that always overwhelmed her at such moments: the feeling of falling in love. Enough of that.

The part of his brain that could still think was holding on to the feeling that always rose at such moments, only to fade as the sweat dried: the feeling of falling in love. He'd never wanted to be a love 'em and leave 'em guy. Enough of that.

They arrived at a pond, a natural one, a tiny, muddy slurp buzzing with the afternoon insects and oozing heavy swamp stink, and as he snorted his relief and excitement, she stepped back from the muddy edge and realized how exhausted she was. Before he waded in, he wanted to be sure no humans were around, so he motioned for her to climb onto his back. She held up her claws to say, I don't want to hurt you. He wriggled his backside to say, We pigs have tough skin, don't let the pink fool you. So she hopped up, craned her neck in every direction and clucked out an all clear. As soon as she was off him, he partly waded, partly rolled, partly melted into the slimy water and her little eyes grew big in a moment of revulsion, giddiness, and vicarious delight.

"This is such a bad idea," Sarah said, still flushed with a satisfaction her boyfriend had so rarely given her, her boyfriend who'd resist his own lust until it overflowed him and he became kind of frantic—and then when it counted was so tentative. This one was so calm, in a way she didn't know was possible, in a way that convinced her that his hands and lips were listening to her and like a good therapist hearing what she couldn't hear herself. And then when it counted, he was just free.

"Why?"

She didn't answer.

Pulling the sheet up over their naked bodies, they fell into a discussion of capitalism. When she described its horrors and dared him to deny it, he laughed and said, "Oh, I don't deny it. In fact, that's not the half of it. But what you don't know is that when you're in it you just feel so alive."

*Do I feel alive?* she asked herself.

"My uncle was a preacher, damning everybody to hell," he said and then stopped himself: *what the hell am I saying?*

"Was? I'm sorry."

"No, he's not dead. He's in jail."

"For what?"

"Tax fraud."

"I thought— "

"So did he."

She wasn't aware that her hand was on his chest and that her finger was running a circle around his hard nipple in the loudly air-conditioned room until he took her hand in his and kissed the back of it as if he were greeting a lady.

At that moment she heard her phone buzzing in her bag and couldn't have cared less for the first time since—since maybe ever.

He turned on the TV and they looked for themselves on the news.

Little Pig rose out of the water, glistening, not exactly clean, but the pond water had washed off the sty filth and he smelled a little better.

Tired as she was, Big Hen stood at the pond's edge, her speckled black breast lovely in the sunlight.

They stared at each other in amazement and at the moment they became aware of their nakedness they heard a car engine not far away. A road, hidden by the trees.

They plunged into the forest again, he carrying her this time, her flapping and going airborne a moment if he stumbled or leapt a twig.

His phone buzzed and he jumped. "That's my wife," he said. He didn't have to say that, and had no idea why he did. Too late now. "We're separated."

"How long?"

"About six hours." He laughed, an awful Republican laugh. And then added, "And three years."

She very quickly imagined a device—maybe a giant dropper, the kind you use for basting a chicken—with which she could remove, to the molecule, the semen now inside her. And then she imagined him putting more in. She covered her eyes with her forearm.

He was in the middle of explaining and she only realized she wasn't listening when she caught the word co-parenting and he said, "Sounds like one of your words, doesn't it."

She was on the pill, no worry there. His people, if they had their way, would have made this moment one of great worry.

He found himself making some kind of plea, the kind he never made, joking about Carville and Matalin, wondering if she'd even heard of them. She still wasn't looking at him.

"I was wrong," she said, removing her forearm from her eyes. "It's not a mistake. In fact it's the most typical thing in the world." She herself was not even sure what she meant.

"It's not typical for me. Usually they're older and married." *Can I not shut myself up?*

"And how am I supposed to feel, proud?"

"I have no idea how anyone is supposed to feel. Least of all myself."

She sat up quickly, and the sheet fell away. He was sitting at the edge of the bed, watching her. He did not glance down at her breasts. He held her gaze and soon started to smile.

"What's more racist," he said, "me assuming they're black or you thrilled they're not?"

She flinched.

"Am I wrong?"

"You're not wrong," she said, and with a tear in her eye, sprang forward and jammed her mouth on his.

They came to a patch of cool moss hardly touched by the late afternoon light. Big Hen jumped off his back and sank into the pillow-soft green in a hazy delirium. Little Pig, full of excitement, found himself scurrying about, peeing on nearby trees, marking them, a signal that any sow would have understood, and while Big Hen could not, when he approached her, champing on his heated saliva, she crouched. She flattened her back.

Chickens have no vaginas and roosters no penises (they mate in what's called a cloacal kiss) and as Little Pig attempted to mount her there was no way around the awful mismatch of their organs. As he tried to enter a place that was never meant to be entered, she clucked pain and fear and blinding desire, and as he sought a depth that he wanted body and soul and that not even cruelty would allow—cruelty that was beyond him anyway—he snorted lust and fear and blinding frustration. It hardly lasted a minute before they gave up.

But it was enough.

Boy and Sarah were dressed and ready to go shortly after night fell, even if neither had any place to be. Her phone hadn't buzzed in three hours. His had buzzed several times but what did he care? She had her yellow leggings back on, he his pig-tail belt.

But the instant he opened the door onto the wet asphalt parking strip where his car stood some thirty feet away, a drizzle turned into a thunder-mad monsoon, as if the cold front marching in from the northwest had been waiting to see their faces.

He thinks: *Is this different? It's always different. Everything is always different and we just don't know it, just like every second is the chance we've been waiting for and what do we do? We just spit into the wind. And what am I now, some philosopher?*

She thinks: *If I had that chicken head here, I'd run all the way back to the Slurp-Mart. I'm 23 and I keep throwing my life away.*

He shuts the door.

"I'm starving," she says.

He takes his phone out and says, "Pizza?"

Big Hen and Little Pig awoke wet and miserable and confused in the morning and wandered forward, hoping the forest would provide.

They didn't last long, but long enough for the miracle to gestate, hatch, and find its way to the chicken coop of a laissez-faire permaculture farmer who didn't mind the large, clumsy, two-toed, nearly featherless rooster with the pinkish comb, who, after overcoming his initial shyness, proved quite popular with the hens. His freakish appearance also got him into many county fairs as well as the pages of several livestock magazines and websites. But these gave no hint of the great role he was destined to play.

Big Hen and Little Pig had both been born with genetic abnormalities including one they shared: the absence of the coding that prevented different species from interbreeding. Thanks to their orphaned love child and his success at mating with genetically typical hens, the spread of this new possibility was begun, and while not fully emerging for millions of years, it would eventually create a bloom of diversity, chaos, and weirdness that would blur if not erase every division in the animal kingdom and yield a display of life beyond anything seen on any planet in the known universe.

Sarah and Boynton lasted a little longer—long enough for her to get pregnant (that damn 0.1%), long enough for him to imply that she should think about ending the pregnancy, which he couldn't say directly given where his party and his people stood (and he as well), and long enough for her to respond with fury at his hypocrisy, though she did not disagree.

The next and last time they spoke, he brought cash to cover the procedure (plus a thousand dollars) and apologized for not being able to accompany her to the clinic. She accepted the envelope but not his apology and ended the encounter (in the same Slurp-Mart parking lot) with as few words as possible. Best to get over him as soon as she could. She jumped into her car and sped away.

He wondered in that moment if he'd ever get over her. He sat in his car a while and then drove slowly home to his wife and kids, with whom he was trying one more time.

# PSYCHO SOCK

## ROBERT WAYNE MCCOY

Rudy, peering out from behind his living room blinds, never would have thought he could feel such rage.

(Listenupi'mtalkingtoyou)

It really wasn't about the garbage but the garbage who owned the trucking company. The guy who owned everything. The guy who made all the rules.

(Themanletsyougetsofarbeforhetakesitawayfromyou)

On his white porch lay several scattered days' worth of newspapers he had failed to pick up. One headline read *Woman Dies in Car Crash With Train*, another, *Wall or no Wall*, and the one on top of the pile, *Lee Handsome Opens Local Gallery*. The last paper made his heart race, fists close, inner thoughts spin like a fidget spinner. The guy who makes the rules.

Just one guy.

*Why is it that I am the only one to see this?* He thought.

(Nottheonlyoneiseeittoo.)

The garbage truck rumbled down the suburban street, a road sentineled by green expanses of lawn, tended trees, and homes. Suburban homes like his own. His reflection stared back at him, black-and-gray-splashed hair, round belly, eyes an early morning blue hue. He heard the beeps of its progress, the hydraulic hum of the press collapsing the week's unwanted bags of scraps. Through his peripheral vision he waited, staring at the curb and his own garbage cans waiting their turn in the cul-de-sac.

(Rememberlastweek)

Yes. Last week. He put out his three cans, one for recycling and two for regular trash. He also put out two more bags of trash that did not fit into the can. One bag he laid on top, the other next to the cans. How much extra effort does it require to just pick those up and throw them in the truck? Instead, the bastard left them on the curb. This week he purposely stuffed his extra bags into the plastic garbage containers, there would be no excuse.

(Rightjustoneb ageneniftheliddidn'tfitperfectly)

*Okay, so he couldn't close the lid over one but surely any reasonable person would just take the damn trash and dump it. I mean that's his job!*

The metallic gray garbage truck sidled up to his curb, stopping a dozen feet beyond the cans. The garbage man jumped off the back and started toward his containers. Beer gut, (Farworsethanyoursofcourse) balding with a red goatee, the garbage guy sauntered over to the cans. Teetering as he walked, a toddler's stroll, he took a moment and flipped off the lid and drug it over to the open back end of the truck and shook free the white plastic bags into the hungry maw. He swung the empty can over onto Rudy's yard and then stopped to look at the second, lidless can. Hand darted onto the top green bag, lifted it out of the can and without looking, dropped it down on the grass.

Rudy felt his teeth grind and face flush in shades of rage as the truck pulled out and back down the street.

(That's right. Listening now, aren't you sweetheart? Go get the gun.)

Rudy's fist clenched, and the rage built as the empty cans and garbage bag filled his view and the garbage truck retreated into next week's pick up. The truck and its logo, *Handsome Sanitation*, receding down the road. (I suppose the man does leave one thing. He leaves people with the shit. Go get the gun, pal!)

Rudy knew he was in a dream, not his own, and one of them was just starting to wake up. Maybe it was time to go see a guy about a gun.

During his children's parties, when he wore his real face, white with a large nose, red wig, he would talk with them and sometimes talk a bit with the sock. Sometimes he remembered what he said. But they laughed.

The children always laughed.

The five steps led down to the shop. Guns on the walls, locked away. Guns on display. Lots of guns. After a few moments of pretending to look, the conversation:

"You need for protection?" said the owner, his gray hair parted in the middle, back slightly bent, hands gnarled and rough.

Rudy nodded.

"Good with firearms?"

Rudy shook his head side to side.

"Then shotgun. Point, spray, and done. Good for home intrusion."

"No."

"Okay. Glock maybe. Fifteen rounds."

"No. I need something else. Something special. Something people say you have."

"People?" said the shop owner. "What people?"

"Doesn't matter. I meet all sorts of people in my line of work. Some of them say you have a special gun. Old. Revolver. And blessed by a priest."

The shopkeeper's face went slack. His tongue licked his dry lips.

"How'd you hear about that?"

"I'm a professional clown. People talk when they're drunk. They talk about other people. They've talked about you."

"Whad they say?"

"Some good some bad, and a bit about the gun. All I care about right now is the gun. Unless you want me to start sharing the bad with other people. Like the police."

"No. No, we good. It's a Colt Barracuda. Holds special .40 caliber rounds. But one bullet only. Only had one in the chamber, when I got it from the guy."

Rudy nodded and said, "That's all I'll need."

Later in the week:

Rudy knew he wanted (make that needed, you drunk) a night out after a day of a horrendous bar mitzvah, leading into an evening of some woman's fortieth birthday party. Not that he turned down the gig, but what husband in their right mind hires a clown for a woman's birthday party? He even heard some of her friends whisper the birthday girl didn't even like clowns. That's some inspiring shit. At least he spent the night harassing the moron husband with jokes, pranks, and fun-filled humiliation. Workday done, it was ten after eleven and Rudy needed that drink, not realizing it might be a confession to which he rode.

B.S., his best friend of ten years, tall, short brown hair, wearing glasses, whose real name was Tony Smak. (With a name like that you would go by B.S. also). A call center manager by profession, but that didn't make him a bad guy. He knew the shit out of beer, hence the B.S. (aka Barley Scholar) honorific his friends referred to him by.

Rudy's clown sense tingled, warning him this conversation was going to suck...

(Just warning: Think before you say it. He has ears everywhere.)

"I'm going to end him."

"Who?"

"Lee Handsome."

"Shit, man, keep it down."

(B.S. is right. You must commit if you want this!)

"Free country."

"Lies, brother. Besides, your plan won't work," B.S. said.

"Why not?" Rudy asked. "I can't be the only one tired of him. People say he's more... not human. I saw the perfect gun."

"Shoot him?"

"Yeah. Colt Barracuda .40 Caliber Revolver. The guy at the gun shop says it actually was used by a saint, some cowboy named MacKindell from the 1860s and was blessed by a priest. Seems like the perfect gun to kill an evil schmuck."

"Maybe, but two counter points. People may think it, but no one says it out loud. He owns the gas stations, the grocery stores, and most of the police. On top of those, he's got our esteemed mayor sitting comfortably in his pocket. He just opened the new gallery."

"Doesn't make it right."

"Yeah. All the wrong reasons add up to just shutting up about it."

(Just let it roll. He already knows. Let this play out. Play him.)

"I can't take the shit anymore, B.S."

"Rudy, he's OG.

"Original gangster? That's cliché."

"No. People in this town consider him the original god, small g. Even has his own adjective. Point two, you're a professionally trained clown, not a Navy SEAL."

"Jester please. Or if you must, auguste white-faced clown. Classically trained."

"Yeah, okay. Classically trained fool. You make people laugh. Handsome, well, he makes people disappear. He owns the city. He owns all of it. You own a clown suit."

(Handsome doesn't own you. You move sideways, Rudy. Maybe can't predict it, or you. You have two faces. And hell, you have me. Go ahead, keep talking....)

"B.S. do you hear that?"

"I hear you. I also hear the silence at the bar from our conversation," B.S. said.

"Okay. Yeah, sorry. This is no joke though. You say clowns aren't tough."

"Umm, yeah."

"What if I was a rodeo clown, Barley?"

B.S. took a long drink of his beer, considered, and said, "They're pretty tough. The odds would have been a bit better."

"My point is people are afraid of clowns," Rudy added between drinking. "I can use that somehow."

"Not with Handsome," B.S. said. "Look, the equation's simple. He's just better at being him than you are at killing people, which, in retrospect... you're probably not so good. That said, rumor is he has a weakness. Beer Flights and a game."

"What?"

"You have to out-fly him."

"I'm a clown not a fighter pilot."

"It's a drinking game, idiot. Four attempts to beat him at a drinking game."

"You believe this?"

"As much as I believe you're a clown."

The two friends laughed. They drank. They talked. That was the last time Rudy would see B.S.

Murder on his mind and in his dreams, the next day found Rudy with a hangover.

The shower called to him, as did the need to shave and eat breakfast. Being Quarterdum the Clown, a favorite of the local area, made him cash; a living, but not millions.

He wanted some eggs and he didn't have any. Rudy decided to make a grocery run. He hoped the Friedman contract would come through today, heaven knows clown makeup isn't cheap. He grabbed a leather jacket from his closet—next to the suit, the wig, the red nose. Jostled from the hanger swinging back, the sock fell. That damned sock fell through the air as if trying to fly. The cheap trick to make children laugh kept falling forever. Rudy turned away closing the door. Somewhere he heard the whisper of a scream.

Palming his fob and phone from his nightstand, he closed his apartment door behind him.

The City, tall spires of steel concrete and glass, stood sentinel over the roads that he drove.

The skyline swirled around the building where Otto Loom lived, like a blur of memory. His penthouse-level home with a terraced roof access. He had purchased it years before, not knowing why he had to have it, only that he must. He went to work in the garbage business and began brewing beer in his tub. Older Otto, balding, thirty years later, in his sixties with his red hair greying. There were buildings that grew around his. Taller, moodier constructs of steel, stone, and concrete. Each story held a different tale, each floor leading to another heart. None of the other stories mattered for shit.

Otto moved a holy man. His mission given by a techno god. He brewed for him.

The drums were sealed and sloshed, their contents weighed and measured. There were four different red sheds, all locked. One with an air conditioner running for his current guest. Mostly, things happened at night. Sometimes people would come to the rooftop. Otto would greet them and see them inside one of the sheds for sanctuary. No outside eyes saw them again. Once the doors closed, they never opened for those interred inside.

The half dozen cats, they stalked the rooftop and slipped inside the building cracks and shadows. If they knew what Otto was doing, they did not say, did not care. This was not a place that wanted attention. It was a lure, a snare, a mousetrap.

Threats were made to be contained, and he to contain them.

As Rudy drove, he saw a message on his phone. He played it back

Hey, it's me, Blayne. Meet me at the new restaurant and brew pub tonight? The Irish Lass? Call me.

Quick note: Blayne was his neighbor, going on a year and a half now. Rudy was not sure exactly what she did for a living, but he thought she worked in an architectural firm. Or a yoga studio? When she was home sometimes, she asked to borrow sugar or laundry soap. Sometimes she asked for more. Rudy didn't mind giving more. He made her laugh when he mentioned shoe size and related it to another body part size. He wore his Quarterdum shoes at the time.

Rudy did call and told Blayne he would meet her at the club. She sounded excited. That usually meant good things for him, or she wanted to ask him for money. Either way, he decided he would chance it.

Rudy lost himself among the cabs and cars, leaving behind all ye boojum and seals while the asphalt-paved miles fell behind him.

Rudy paid for parking and looked around the garage. Various cars were tucked into parking spaces, the city noises symphonic and projected into the cement structure; and a gray and white seagull stood on a third-story ledge looking at him. Rudy started for the elevator. The gull's head seemed to swivel and follow him. When he looked back, waiting for the doors to open, it winged away.

The club was a converted factory that had made buggy whips nearly a hundred years ago. The front entrance offered a water view of a battle-worn and permanently docked aircraft carrier that was now an exclusive club and museum, formerly the battle-hardened USS Intrepid. Rudy sauntered along the sidewalk, offering a hello to the over-steroid-using and sunglasses-wearing bouncer. Arms crossed, the brute glared down and nodded behind the shades, and Rudy walked inside.

Inside, waterfalls fell and Irish music rose, the recreation of a town with store fronts and painted vistas of the perfect

Emerald Isle town. Road leading to the Lass, of course, where the music played, and the beer flowed, and the waitress had nice big ... clovers.

Speaking of clovers, Rudy waded through the crowd and found her at the bar. Legs crossed, velvet miniskirt on, red hair tossed to one side, she already had ordered two beers. That was part of their thing. They always tried new microbrews when they went out. He leaned against the bar with a smile. Blayne leaned over and gave Rudy a nice long kiss. She had that bright gloss on, the type that claims the color lasts twenty-four hours, which sort of felt like a personal challenge. Mid-kiss, Rudy noticed her eyes roll to a few suits playing pool off to the side of the bar, tucked in the corner away from the band. She pulled away. Rudy thought he might be getting into trouble. Another kiss like the last one, now tasting of beer and he might not mind.

"Hey," she said.

"Nice." Rudy took another drink from the glass. Had a pine taste to it, like the west coast beers.

"The beer? Or the kiss?"

She licked her top lip, slowly, playfully.

"Yes. More of both please."

She laughed, ran her hand through her auburn hair. He liked her laugh. In a job where he made a living making people laugh, when someone gave that back to him, it was special. She took a drink but didn't offer the second kiss.

"Who're the suits over there?" Rudy asked.

"You don't want to know."

"If I didn't, I wouldn't have asked."

"I'll get to them."

Serious; her voice sounded serious.

"You in trouble, Blayne?"

"Maybe. But not as much as you."

Rudy stopped mid-swallow, staring at her over the rim of the half-full beer glass. He saw the suits, ladies setting down their cue sticks on the table. The first of them wearing sunglasses in the dim and shadowy bar, started to walk over. One shambled, towering nearly seven feet and rail thin, rocking a crew cut. The other heavy, possessed of blocky frame, with a long ponytail and round glasses like John Lennon had worn. They flanked a man who joined them in their walk.

"Lovely beer. A microbrewery from the west coast. B.S would love it," she said. "Too bad he can't be here."

"Who are they, Blayne?"

"Tall one is Mrs. Yin. The other, Miss Yang. They're professionals."

"Professional what?"

Blayne shrugged. Offered next a weak, half-smile, saying nothing; saying everything.

"Shit. What have you done?" Rudy asked.

"I'm sorry. I owe him. He made me call you. They work for him."

"Who made you call?"

Blayne leaned closer. In the bar, with the noise, Rudy felt her breath tickle the hairs on his ear. "The man who tricked the Devil."

"Who?"

"Oh, he's a lot of people. Some people, though, call him the Pumpkin King behind his back. He likes Burgers and Beer. He prefers being called...

That hit Rudy, a sledgehammer trying to slam its way from the inside of his head-out. He said, interrupting her... "Mr. Handsome."

"Yup."

# (The Devastating Lee Handsome)

"The man himself. The main man."

"Oh, oh no!"

"Yeah, Right? He's real. This is his place. (Of course, it is…) The real deal and he has a proposal for you."

Rudy drank the last of his beer and ordered another as the women walked away. The man stopped and spoke with another table, the three men sitting there suddenly attentive and swept away by the presence of the man taking the time to speak to them. They all laughed as the suit-wearing women blocked his view. A lingering moment passed, and the conversation was excited by the two ladies. They continued the walk toward him and Blayne. Both wore matching gray suits, red ties, black shoes.

"Good afternoon." Miss Yang said.

Rudy nodded.

"Our employer would like to speak with you," Mrs. Yin said.

"About?"

"Simple. You want to kill him, but there are rules. And a game to be played."

"I don't play games."

The voice soft and controlled, Mrs. Yang said, "But you're a clown?"

"That, madam, is all business."

From the other table Lee Handsome, made his exit and started toward Rudy.

A waitress found the table first. Instead of the beer he had ordered she carried a board, decorated in Halloween pumpkin design. On top of it was a double flight of smaller beers. The lightest microbrew, a pilsner to the right, followed by an India Pale Ale, a porter, and a dark stout. She set the board upon the table, careful not to spill a drop.

Mr. Handsome waved the women away. Blayne went with them. Her eyes held Rudy's own. Fear glistened in them. She slipped away. Only he and Handsome remained.

"I like that: Quarterdum. I like that very much. King know about your name? Guess it doesn't matter. Mind if I sit?"

"Your table."

He sat. Red hair, freckles, tall, and he spoke with an Irish lilt. "I've a game to offer. One we can both win. You save your friend from his containment. And..."

"Friend?"

"B.S. He's being transmuted. It's science. Like brewing. You don't have much time." Handsome reached into his inside jacket pocket and withdrew a .40 caliber six shooter. That sandal-worn grip aged but smooth, the gun metal cared for and immune to time's rust. Ancient, aged from the 1860s or 70s. He had bought it a few days ago. Handsome left it upon the table.

"Sorry, had my girls get it from your house. You know, some holy guy owned this, named MacKindell. A real life Saint."

"The story's true?"

"Sure. Imagine Clint Eastwood's swagger, but not an actor. Real life badass. Walked with a bible and gun, like those U2 and Johnny Cash song lyrics said."

"It's true then?"

"True as anything else, laddie. True as a blessed bullet."

Rudy took the gun. Opened the cylinder and saw the bullet, slapped it back in place. He palmed the handle, rifled barrel leveled at Handsome.

"You're evil. Something ancient and sinister about you. Why don't I just end you and do the world a favor?"

Handsome laughed.

"I would love that, but it doesn't work. Believe me, I've tried. I need to do it by losing a game. Choose wisely, Quarterdum."

His thumb slid the hammer back with a satisfying click.

Handsome grinned and said, "One blessed bullet. Don't waste it."

Rudy's raised the gun to the man's right eye.

(It won't work. Not yet. Flight or fight the usual rule but this time only flight. Challenge him or B.S dies.)

His finger curled around the trigger, it slowly, lovingly drawing back...

"Choose, Mr. Quarterdum."

Shaking, his finger released.

"Flight," he whispered.

"Now we're talking. Drink up. It's an East Coast Pilsner. Call it Shine a Lite. German Malt with hints of yogurt with American hops. A good start to the game."

Rudy stared at the words, hanging in the air. The waitress approached the table with the board and the flight. Rudy felt a chill fill the room – also on the table was the damned sock. It lay on its side, one visible button eye staring at him. The smile woven into the heel, matching Mr. Handsome's...

"Why this, Handsome? Why the game?"

"Not a game, Rudy. Ritual. It's needed for the psyche, or if you rather, the soul. Rituals like Halloween. Or friends getting together for drinks. Or a priest blessing the bullets of an ancient gun." He grinned pumpkin wide, raised his glass and said, "Salud."

Together they drank the first round of beer, and it began.

The city skyline moved around the building where Otto Loom lived, swaying like a blur of memory. Each story held a different tale, each floor leading to another heart. None of the other stories mattered for shit.

Otto brewed. He brewed things. He used people. It was all that he ever loved.

The pilsner done. A second beer, an IPA. Carmel colored, lots of sharp notes and flowery.

"Sip it and tell me about it."

Rudy sipped. He tasted. "Hints of grapefruit and guava. Very drinkable."

"Right. I agree. I see B.S. trained you well. Round one, done. Now for the first contest. Make me laugh, Rudy."

Rudy considered and said, "What did one DNA strand say to the other strand?"

Handsome shrugged and drank from the IPA-filled glass. It was light in color, liquid swirling, amber joy.

Rudy said, "Do my genes make me look fat?"

Handsome did laugh.

After the chuckles subsided, he said, "Here's a joke, and I bet you laugh. What do you do if a wild pack of clowns attacks you, Rudy?"

"Go for the juggler."

"Wrong. You kill a Quarterdum."

They both laughed and downed their glasses.

He was certain there were a few neighbors, those more meddlesome, who wondered why a shed needed an air conditioner. Perhaps they wondered why he had so many containers.

Sometimes people would come to the rooftop. Otto would greet them and see them inside one of the sheds for sanctuary. No eyes saw them again. Once the doors closed, they never opened for those interred inside. No human eyes remained. There were the cats, they stalked the rooftop and slipped inside the building. If they knew what Otto was doing, they did not say. Cats never say.

This was not a place that wanted attention. It was a lure, a snare, a mousetrap.

Otto held a pair of oversized shoes. He placed them in the soaking liquid, held in a special drum. They represented so much.

The drums were sealed and their contents sloshed, weighed, and measured. There were four different sheds, all locked. One, painted on the inside with a dark brown stain, with an air conditioner humming. B.S. saw the drum, the liquid filling it. The liquid smelled a lot like a good oatmeal stout beer.

B.S. felt rough hands draw him toward the drum. Otto was strong, and he loved his work. B.S. heard a laugh tumble down from the future.

"Wait please...no."

Otto grinned at him and said, "There's only waiting now. The purifying and the bright tank for you."

"Please. It's not my fault."

Otto picked him up and dangled B.S. over the lip of the drum. He said "I know. It's your friend's fault, his trash talk. Mr. Handsome now deals with that. While I … get you."

And B.S. fell into the water that was not beer. It was a trick. It was an offering. He felt something press against his side already placed in the liquid. He screamed as the liquid encompassed him.

With the sun and its fading light framing the sheds, the rooftops remained quiet. The drums sat in the darkness.

Elsewhere a man and his drinking partner, two beers set aside, the third in hand, and a game in the playing.

"Round two. Your friend's in trouble. The Stout is called Shout into The Darkness. Notes of fig and biscuit and chestnut. Alchemy is a science of myth and legend. Brewing is part of this unique art. Tell me how much you have learned from your friend B.S.?"

"What do you mean?"

"About Beer. Brewing?"

"We've talked."

"Good. I also brew things. I have a brew master who uses everything from people. Their ideas, their bodies, their clothes. It's like Halloween. All full of tricks or treats."

"Like this damn game."

"Just like a sock" Handsome said. And how he smiled.

The chocolate flavored, dark brew awaited them.

(Let it all go Rudy. You know it was me they always wanted to see) said the sock looking up at Rudy on the table.

"Round three, Rudy."

"Must be the beer. Something wrong with it. Drugged me," Rudy said. The world spun. Far too fast for just four beers...

(No. It's the truth. You have always been mine. I wore you like face paint, a nose, and a funny suit, Quarterdum. But please note what's happening now, what you choose to see and get involved in is bigger than you and me and Blayne and B.S. It will change the world. Mr. Handsome will change it. So, you see, I am sorry. I really am. Now do the right thing and let's have one more performance.)

The sock's hand and mouth, named Rudy, shouted, "This is insane. I'm talking to a sock!"

(Now you know how I have felt for years. Being stuck with a clown. Now, man up and smile!)

The sock said out loud "It's all about sacrifice. Life, I mean. A pistol sacrifices a bullet. A friend sacrifices for a friend. An ancient pistol sacrifices an ancient man. We all must decide. That's how the game is played."

Mr. Handsome slid the pistol across the table.

The sock slipped the hand inside it, letting flesh fill, and flex, and move.

Mr. Handsome picked up the third beer of the flight. What Rudy held in his hand was dark and stout; as dangerous as a beer.

"Do you save B.S. or yourself?" Mr. Handsome asked, his voice distant and lost. Both the OG and the sock smiled at him. He put something to his lips, not certain if it was a beer or a barrel. He thought maybe they were in this instance one in the same. Maybe it was the start of his own personal flight.

The sock moved Rudy's finger around the trigger.

Thunder sounded, and a blessed bullet flew.

Blayne laughed, short and choppy. It was not the funny kind of laughter at all. No, it was the complete and terrible opposite. She walked out alone, the bar light flickering off the sock on her right hand. The sock was smeared in shadow and in wet red. She ran the down the street feeling so light on her feet she began to fly.

Blayne flew right toward a car's oncoming headlights...

B.S. woke on the street outside of the Irish Lass. He remembered floating. Not in water but in time and space. He remembered the sound of wings of something terrible coming, something flying this way to a trap, and Otto and his master, Mr. Handsome, the old god waiting for it, waiting to greet it.

The drums full of beer to entice a bigger game. The drum tipping over, spilling him back to the cold of his body and the concrete floor. Everything had changed and he the least of it.

B.S. staggered down the street still hearing the wings of something coming. Something horrible to end the world. A terror that Mr. Handsome was calling forth with the sound of trapped people screaming in those special drums. And the promise of a special brew.

And all he cared about was getting a damn beer. A beer could save him or at least make him forget...

Lee Handsome drank the last beer alone. This game all but done, this flight all but crashed and burned. But hell, at least the beer tasted good; and that was sometimes all the luck an Irishman could ask.

At least until the next game. The end game.

The Devastating Lee Handsome smiled and called for another beer.

(Okay, you, the one reading this. Yeah, you. The gift from Otto didn't work so well for Rudy or B.S. or Blayne; but if you have need to walk somewhere, anywhere, I know I would be a good fit. Sometimes you must walk in another man's clown shoes. Just let me know, we can talk about it. I might even have a joke or two...)

# DEATH'S AUCTION

## KELLY HEINEN

Death is for sale. From funerals, to transporting the bodies, to fancy caskets, there's money to be made. I work for two sides of death: by day, I transport bodies to funeral homes, morgues, even state labs. But by night, I transport spirits to the other side. And that 'other side' just went on the market. That may not seem like a big deal, but this is the first time in two hundred years The One True Death has no heir. Not one person who is in line to take over. Horace, the current company head, never married and never had kids, but he also never planned to retire.

I suppose it's nice having immortality on your side.

But things happen, and he apparently got the Death equivalent of a pink slip, stating that after two hundred years, it was time to pass the scythe. With no heir, his job is up for sale, and it's attracted a lot of bidders. The Death industry is lucrative. And taking over as the One True Death means a lot of money.

Even in Death, money talks. It influences who moves up or down the chain of command, and it's used to convince the living Deathers that there's more money in their night hustle than in their real-world jobs. Many Deathers stay on after their year of service is over because of the money. Of course, it's an industry that never dies. Without it, the current overpopulation problem would become a literal nightmare.

I'm one of the Deathers for Iowa, and Horace, who oversees everybody, no matter where they work, is my boss. Normally the top job is passed down to an heir. This has created an issue, and for reasons unknown, Horace set his sights on me. He's also the one who started the current mess because he thought the easy way out was to offer me the top job. I said no thank you, the robes don't even come in my size, and thought that would be the end of it. Of course, it doesn't work that way. Horace is very... well, let's just say that when I turned the job down, he said 'there are *rules*, Carla.' Basically, he told me I couldn't say no. And pointed out that the robes do, actually, come in fluffy sizes.

Once he realized I wasn't having it, he heaved a sigh as heavy as a burial vault and explained that the job would go up for sale. This wasn't an issue to me, until I started meeting some of the interested parties. And believe me, every single underling in the Death industry is interested. Every country has their Head Death, and then Deathers trickle down in seniority from there. Most of the Head Deaths have been fairly pleasant, if a bit confused that I'm not Horace's actual heir. But some of them are aggressive and figure that by being a bully they'll net the ultimate victory. Instead, Horace plans to award it to the highest bidder at an auction at the end of the year, but the bullies might be in for an unpleasant surprise.

The corn fields of Iowa, more than knee-high now that it's mid-July, sail past in a blur as I fly over them, giving my horse, Destiny, a chance to stretch her legs. We circle the water tower in my hometown of Larchwood, and Destiny skims the tassels off a row of corn. As I watch her hooves expertly de-tassel the stalks, my laugh echoes over the town. When I think of the sweaty summers I spent pulling those stubborn things off and she pops them with ease! I pull up on her reins so I can snap a picture of the Milky Way.

No, it's not normal for horses to fly. But she has some kind of mojo on her and is only happy when she's flying. Flying over Iowa is so beautiful, especially in the summer. There's no stress, the air is warm, and the sunsets are magnificent. Being a courier of the dead to the other side, I don't get to do this often. But when I get a night off, I take full advantage.

*Incoming*

*Huh?*

I appreciate my boss trying to be supportive, but sometimes he's more confusing than helpful. But an almost supersonic whooshing noise makes my head throb, and I slam my palms over my ears. Good god, what is that thing?

*That is Death Portugal. Quite a pompous thing, if you ask me. I have not enjoyed his company, and I do not think you will, either.*

The snap of bones is overshadowed by a sucking noise as the condor morphs into a human.

*He totally just shape-shifted. Is this dude human?*

*I believe you would describe him as -ish, if I remember your wording from the other day.*

*What did I describe as -ish?*

*I believe it was the weather. You said it was cold-ish for July.*

*Oh. That. Well, can someone be human-ish?*

*Of course. Perhaps not in your normal human world, but in the Death world there are many possibilities in this regard.*

Refocusing my attention, I quirk an eyebrow. The grin on the shape-shifter is certainly human. When the final feather is gone, the naked man shakes himself, then my horse drops down to avoid a fireball.

Electricity sparks between my fingers and I throw a lightning bolt in retaliation. I have never had a Deather hit me with a fireball before they say hello. "Why the hell did you start a fight?"

"I am placing my bid for the job of One True Death. Therefore, we must meet in battle and fight to the death."

Oh, Hell no! I grip my scythe in my left hand, Destiny's reins in my right. Closing my eyes, I focus on the scythe, charging it until it crackles. When I open my eyes, Death Portugal seems to be reconsidering this fight. Too late now, I'm pissed off.

*You are most fierce when angry. Perhaps I should warn potential bidders of this fact.*

*Don't you dare.*

Horace goes quiet, but the mental link we share remains open. He's probably watching to see who wins. If I have any say in the matter, Portugal is going to limp home with his wings between his talons.

"Perhaps we can talk?" His thick, accented voice booms over me and I flinch. Damn, that dude is loud.

Taking a deep breath, I try to ignore the ringing in my ears. Destiny's ears twitch and her head shakes, making me hold on tight. She's thrown me before, and trust me, it hurts when I slam into her saddle lady parts first.

"Fuck that! You struck first."

I point my scythe tip, but he sprouts wings faster than my lightning bolt can fly. His wings shake the air as he swoops low, my bolt missing by a mile. Destiny rears as a fireball nicks her back leg and I hang on for dear life. Unlike my opponent, I can't sprout wings. Being the fluffy gal I am, I will drop like a rock and land with a splat.

"You touch my horse, you will regret it!"

A fireball flies from my hand and nails Portugal in the chest. He's half-condor now but instead of a screech, he snorts at me, as if his nose is full of snot or something. That's not intimidating. Trying not to let my high-pitched giggle loose, I regain my saddle and recharge my scythe.

"If I take over, I make more money. More money means raises for my staff, which they will appreciate. It is in your best interest to let me take over."

Yep, there's money in death at all levels. My boss pays a minimum of one thousand dollars per crossover, depending on how quickly I bring them across. There are bonuses if I complete my list early every night, for the age of my crossover. And if I happen to snag an extra soul or two in the process, that also brings in extra. There are always unexpected deaths, at least to the families, but those of us in charge of the hourglasses know better.

"Yeah, yeah, yeah, it's all about the fucking money. No decision has been made and I don't understand why you want to fight me for it. You take this shit up with Horace."

"You are the reluctant heir. Therefore, my fight is with you."

On a whim, I wave my hand and a shield snaps into place over myself and Destiny. Portugal lobs a glowing green ball of energy at us, with a tail like a comet. The ball bounces harmlessly off us, and I follow up with a ball of lightning that singes his left wing. Bones snap and re-form and soon, he's full man again -- or -ish, as Horace said. Panting, I wait him out, another fireball ready in my hand.

He blinks, floating there above the earth, like it's the most natural thing in the world. Finally, feathers reform on his arms. His bones snap and reposition themselves and then, with a deafening snort, he spreads his wings. The whoosh of his wings makes me go momentarily deaf, and I wonder how it sounds to the humans below.

He flies off and leaves me with my mouth hanging open. I cough when a bug takes a nosedive into my throat, and I swear Destiny laughs. Coughing and sputtering, I take a moment, blinking at the stars.

"Dude, what the fuck just happened?"

Not that horsey thoughts are very helpful, but Destiny flaps her wings in what I imagine is a shrug. Turning the scythe tip southward, I aim at the star Antares. The sky distorts for a second and then a tunnel opens, busy with Deathers going back and forth across the Dark Plane. The walls are made of connective membranes, like the synovial membranes that keep joints moving, and they bend and fold as we walk on the stone floor. The tunnel feels alive, light pulsing through the hollow, round, deep purple veins that run along the membranes. Nodding to a couple as I pass, we make top speed to Horace's desk.

"Carla, Destiny, well done on your fight. I see you have finally learned to stay in your saddle."

My pelvis gives a throb, as if to remind me of my tumbles. During recent training exercises, Horace had Destiny stop, drop, and roll while I learned to dodge attacks and attack in return. Staying in my saddle was a serious challenge and my nimble horse caught me more than once feet above the ground.

I grip my scythe and bang the rough stone floor. The office shakes, and Horace's bony fingers grip his smooth, oak desk. If he was in his human form, he'd have blinked.

"I can't believe you let Portugal beat me up without intervening!"

"I must say, you performed most admirably."

My scythe shakes the room again, Horace's desk momentarily levitating. He stands, reaching for the sharp blade on a stick, but I hold fast.

"I don't appreciate battles with bullies." My glare tracks him as he approaches, Destiny nudging my shoulder with her snout. Normally that calms me down but not today.

His feet clack on the cold stone as he paces a moment, then turns back to me. The problem with my temper is that it can turn a nice, sunny day into one that's tempest-tossed and tornadic. His next words very likely cause the team at the National Weather Service in Sioux Falls to start drinking. Again.

"There is nothing I can do. The bidders are excited. Therefore, despite being asked to maintain their manners, some bidders are willing to fight to the death for the top spot. You will simply have to deal with them."

His office door might be an eight-foot-thick concrete slab with ornate carvings and gold inlays, but it still slams. The entire Dark Plane shakes as I stomp toward the tunnel and wrench it open with the point of my scythe. Destiny fast-trots behind me, ducking through the portal before it closes. The tunnel shakes as we near the skies over Iowa, and if it weren't for Destiny getting ahead of me, I'd have walked right out into nothing and dropped.

*Do come back, Carla*

Telepathy can be such a pain in the ass sometimes. Slamming a mental shield up, I scan the skies for that damn condor. We're not finished, and I intend to let him know it. Destiny whinnies when a sonic whoosh fills the skies. This time I'm prepared and cover my ears before he gets any closer. A pair of moldable ear plugs wink into my hand and I groan; of course Horace is paying attention. Nonetheless, I pop them in, then wait for Portugal to finish shifting.

"Back for more?" he asks, his accent teasing. His beady black eyes run me over and I charge my scythe as he grins.

"Might ask the same of you."

His hand glows orange and I fire off my first ball of lightning. Destiny drops, and his energy ball misses. The shield snaps into place over us, a momentary blue glow the only clue that something has happened. When he throws a fireball, I counter with my own. Below, a pop-up thunderstorm churns, fueled by my temper.

Portugal leers at me. "You fight well. You will be a fine retention to the team."

Lightning zips between us while bigger bolts stretch from ground to cloud below. The clouds twist and churn, and I raise my hand, as if scooping up sand. Instead, the clouds bend, bringing the funnel up. Portugal's face twists in shock as my hand cocks and throws, wind buffeting us both. His wings spawn even as he tumbles away, head over heels.

*Nice move. That is not something I taught you.*

I discard the funnel and Destiny surges forward, a bolt of lightning hot in my hand. I find him sitting in the ladle of the Big Dipper, one leg crossed over the other, long fingers curled over the edges of the cup. A thought morphs my bolt into a ball and I lob it toward him. His hand deflects it, and it rolls placidly up one side of the ladle and down the other before settling in the middle.

A smirk pulls at the corner of his mouth. "I have placed my bid, why do you continue this fight? Practice? A secret desire to take the job after all? If you wish the job, it is yours; no one will fight you for it, because Horace picked you first."

His tone drips with sarcasm, that smirk infuriating me. A ball of fire bounces languidly in his hand, his condor holding steady. Tension sizzles between us as he holds my gaze, cocky as ever. My fighting hand dangles at my side, Destiny at a dead stop. The storm below dissipates as I consider his words. I don't care who has the job, as long as it's not me. I'm ready to go back to being a normal human being. Or as close as I can get, after this last year of bringing people into their afterlife. If I'm being honest, I'm not even sure I *am* human anymore.

"You are speechless, young Deather," he continues.

He hops down and for once his wings are quiet as he floats. He's far enough away that I could pierce him with one well-placed lightning bolt. But my temper has subsided. Below, the clouds are gone, the storm already a distant memory for most folks.

"Why did you attack me?" I ask.

His wings are hands and arms again and he spreads them, with a shrug. "It is the way of things. Did Horace not prepare you for this? That once his job went up for sale there would be a vicious auction?"

"He only said there would be an auction. It seems to me he thought most people would be polite and not giant assholes. Fairly sure the highest bidder would also be the most polite." There's a split-second spark in my hands before I take a deep breath. Portugal watches with interest, his eyes focused on my every move; a sly grin never leaves his face.

"Be that as it may, Death is a hot commodity. Therefore, many of us are willing to acquire it at whatever cost. If that cost is what you deem poor manners, then it is a trivial concern. To rule a global empire that controls the humans is a dream for many."

Floating above those humans, I take another deep breath. "Are you human?"

The grin turns into a smirk. He shifts one arm into a wing, then back to an arm. "Am I?" Crackling energy seems to growl around my left hand. He raises one hand and I take another breath. "No, dear, I am not. Should any human look inside me, they would think themselves crazy." He idly tosses a fireball from one hand to the other before holding it up for me to see. "Do you really believe a human could do the things we do?"

I scoff, as Destiny adjusts her position. "Of course not. I'm not stupid."

He saunters closer and my horse backs up. No human can walk on thin air, either. Whatever his purpose, he's intense about it. He closes the gap between us. Destiny gives him a warning snort, her mane flying. A black cloud forms below us, my left hand still crackling.

"You are not human, either." He snaps his fingers and my shield falls. I fling a ball of lightning at him. Thunder rumbles, lightning stretching from cloud to ground. "That temper of yours is certainly not human. Why do you fight so quickly?"

The tunnel opens to let Horace through, his sleek black steed Zarathustra standing some forty hands high. For a moment, Portugal gulps, but his swagger resumes and he retrieves my previous fireball from the Big Dipper. He lobs it at Horace, who extinguishes it before it gets close.

"Your bid is forfeit, Portugal."

Didn't see that coming. The two immortals square off, condor to horse and skeleton. The condor's beak morphs into the tip of a scythe while Horace wields his enormous black blade. In a blur of feathers, Portugal cracks Horace's upper left arm. The clouds below churn and crackle, thunder a constant symphony as I lob three bolts into the feathers of the overgrown bird. Horace is healed in seconds and Portugal freezes in place.

"You will be exiled for a period of one day to the Silent Plane. After that time, you may rejoin us and attempt another bid."

Portugal shakes himself as a vortex opens to his left, and a deafening wind pulls him inside. It whooshes closed and I turn to face Horace. His bony hands grip the reins of his steed.

"How--?" I blink at him, mouth hanging open.

He shrugs, and the tunnel back to the Dark Plane opens. "I thought about it and it happened. He will be back and I will have a meeting with him. At that time, he can decide if he wishes to play nice, as it were, or if he wishes to continue to be rude and demanding. If he chooses to play by the rules, his bid will be permitted. I have not actually forfeited his bid, but he knows it is a strong threat. Immortals have different rules than humans."

He turns to leave, but I stop him. "One more question. He said I'm not human. Is that true?"

A moment of silence speaks volumes. The storm has dissipated once again. I wait for his answer. It's not often Horace is nervous, being the one in charge of Death, but now he fidgets, one hand lightly resting on his horse's mane. I bite my lip, trying to keep my emotions in check; I consider myself a strong person and I refuse to cry over this. Nonetheless, the longer he remains silent, the more my heart breaks and tears threaten. Damn him.

"You were, when you began working for me." Horace pauses, stroking Zarathustra's mane. If he had eyes, I imagine they'd be darting back and forth. The little fires that burn in his eyes morph from blue to red to orange and back to blue. With a heave of his shoulders, he delivers the final blow. "But... in order to perform your job... you require powers beyond the capabilities of a human. Therefore, you could not remain human." He pauses for a moment. "I am sorry if that bothers you, Carla. But it was imperative. A human would die the first time they used the powers you have."

"Oh."

For a second, my brain rattles, shaken. All this time I've wanted to quit this job, go back to a normal life. But would I have a normal life anymore? Gah! I have so many questions and Horace floats there, looking for all the world like telling someone they're not human anymore is normal. Then again, after two hundred years in his job, maybe it is normal. Massaging my temples, I meet his empty gaze, the little fires in his sockets a calming blue. Cursing myself for being weak, I fight back tears. Dad taught me a long time ago that girls don't cry over much.

"So... if I leave the Death industry--?"

He inclines his head, regarding me. "Well—you would return to your regular life. But I am afraid the changes are permanent. I can, of course, turn off your powers, as it were, but I cannot return you to human. Your body has adapted and changed to accommodate your abilities. Walking between Earth and the Dark Plane, for instance, has changed the makeup of your cells. A doctor would look inside you and see nothing amiss; a closer look would show significant changes. Even those who return to the human way of life are forever changed from their time as Deathers."

That message got through loud and clear: You can quit, but you're never really done. The job stays with you. Well, shit. There's a part of me that knew about the changes, but having it all verified is another thing all together. Sighing, I lean forward, my hand languidly moving up and down Destiny's neck.

"I still don't want the job."

"That is fair. But you will stay on?"

Shoulders momentarily slumping, I grip Destiny's reins. She shakes her head, wings fluttering as she prepares to take our leave.

"I don't see that I have a choice."

"I shall inform the council."

He leaves, and I float. Where have the last couple hours gone? Destiny takes me home, our mental link conveying my wishes before I even know I have them.

After I stable and feed her, I walk into my house, my robes and scythe already stowed somewhere in the ether between home and the Dark Plane. Poking my arm, I feel flesh and bone, muscle and a little fluff, too. Not human, huh? I sure as hell feel human. Exhausted, I go up to bed, stopping to brush my teeth. Those feel human, too. Crawling into bed, I huff out a breath. I can still smell the recent rain.

*Good night, Carla.*

I turn out the lights and shut my human-feeling eyes. Maybe I should reconsider my position. If my humanity has already been stolen, what's left?

# Coming in 2020

## Dark Star Warrior:
## The Morian Treasure

R.S. Mellette

When I first met Kiya, I wasn't the galactic adventuress that I am today. I was simply Nadir Alotus, daughter of the famous Sir Janus Alotus. Don't get me wrong, he was my Dad, and I loved him and Mom very much, but sometimes it was hard to live in his shadow before I had a shadow of my own.

I was kind of a geek back then. This wasn't my fault. I was in my first fifteenth of life, and Dad was a diplomat, so being his little girl was like being royalty-geek. I was going to state dinners as soon as I was old enough to use my own knife and fork. I talked like a midlife college professor. I was raised to be prim, proper, and protocolish. The me back then would bore the me today to death. But what did I know? I was the only kid from Caseri, my native planet, living on Victalus, the world where I grew up, so I spent most of my time with Mom and Dad.

Then, when Mom died...

I don't want to talk about that. She died of space plague, which is to say, any one of the viruses, bacteria, or whatever from one of the planets she and Dad visited. It took her a long time to die, it wasn't pretty, and it still makes me sad to think about, so that's all I'm saying about that for now.

Mom's funeral was kind of a funny scene when I think about it now.

You have to picture all of these formal Victalusites gathered together at an event they knew nothing about. They must be the most uptight beings in the universe. They conform to the Evolution of Sentient Life Theory – they are symmetrical with articulate fingers, triangulating sensory receptors (you know: at least two eyes, two ears, etc.), and big brains like the rest of us.

But beyond that, Victalusites show little sign of actual life and this follows them in death. Alive, they wear clothes that wrap them so tight they can barely breathe and cover them from chin to toes. They must have bladders big enough to hold an ocean, 'cause... well, let's just say there are a lot of buttons. In death, they are just as retentive. The bodies are cremated in some factory, while the friends and family sit around the house drinking tea and not talking to each other or showing any emotion.

On Caseri, we bury our dead. Mom often talked about visiting her parents' graves on the coast. They died when she was about as old as I am now, so they never got to see her graduate from school, meet Dad, get married, have me, or any of the other important stuff in life. Mom said it helped her to go there and talk with them. It helped her work things out. She made Dad promise that I'd have a place to visit her, so he arranged for her burial in our favorite place on Victalus, a meadow under a big shade tree.

Anyway, the locals did the best they could with a very formal funeral for my very informal Mom. Out of respect for my father's work, visitors from all over the galaxy gathered for the solemn ceremony. I didn't know any of them except my friend Kuwn. His family were refugees from Admiral Ghen's invasion of their home planet, Grasa. None of them talked much about it, but Ghen was famous for doing horrible things to the worlds he captured. It must have been true, because I could see a deep kind of sadness in Kuwn's eyes.

So, there were the tightly wrapped Victalusites and formal visitors from distant planets gathered for Mom's funeral, when from over a distant hill walked the wildest bad-ass I had ever seen. If I'd not spent another minute with her, just the sight of her confident strut would have changed my life forever.

Kiya was under-dressed and over-armed for the occasion, wearing thigh-high leather boots – one of which held her switchblade – and a black pressure suit made of Nano-Leather that looked like a corset of straps in strategic places. Strategic for blood flow that is. When you're pulling G-forces, positive or negative, the Nano-stuff figures out what body parts to squeeze so you don't blackout, or red-out depending on the pressure. Of course I didn't know any of that when Kiya walked over the hill. I just thought she was there to kill someone.

Most space jocks wore their pressure suits under their regular clothes as underwear, but not Kiya. Often that was all she wore. Well, that and her pistol slung low on her thigh, some funky jewelry that always included a matching set of ear cuffs, and sunglasses with an orange tint to them. She had a mane of shaggy, golden brown hair that seemed to lighten or darken with every move she made. It was long and full, but never got in her way. All of this adorned a body that I wish I had. Boys must have loved her though her attitude reeked of "you touch, you die." I got the feeling she could back that attitude with action.

Apparently, Kiya didn't come for the funeral. She waited a polite distance away while a priestess finished her speech about the sacred flow of Time.

"Now, if you have an offering, or would like to say some private words with the deceased, please step forward." The priestess gestured for us to line up. Dad was first, so he put his offering into Mom's grave and waited for me to do the same. I put in mine – a letter I had written for her and a bracelet I'd made her when I was in my first fifth. She had taught me how to make it while she shared memories of being a girl on Caseri. I thought she might like something that reminded her of home. I told her that I would love her forever. It was hard. She looked so lonely in there by herself.

Dad placed his hand on my shoulder. "You okay?"

I wasn't, but I nodded yes anyway, wiped my eyes and put on my best brave face.

"Good. I need to speak with someone, but I'll be right back."

He went to talk to Kiya, leaving me to play sad hostess to a bunch of people I barely knew. But I would have none of that. I made a show of a deep sigh, wandered off like I needed to be alone and sat on a little rocky outcrop, a perfect place to listen in on Dad's conversation.

"Sir Janus Alotus, I presume," said Kiya. Her voice was smooth.

"You're Kiya?"

"What can I do for you?"

"You've heard of me?" asked Dad.

"Are you the mouthpiece that's trying to unite the planets and get a peace treaty with the pirate systems?"

"I'm afraid so."

"Then I've heard of you." She was cool. Very cool.

"I imagine I'm not so popular among your friends." Dad was a master of understatement.

"I haven't got any friends, but there is a price on your head." She paused for a second to see his reaction.

During that little pause, I tried to figure out exactly what color her hair was. Each individual strand seemed to have its own shade, from blonde, to light red, dark red, brown, and black. The combination made it look tan from a distance, but it would change with the light or how it blew in the wind – or maybe her mood. I wasn't sure, but I was jealous. My mousy brown hair could never compete with hers.

While I mused briefly about her hair, Dad glanced around at his ever-present security team. I think the mention of the pirate reward for his capture spooked him a little.

"Don't worry," said Kiya. "I'm no bounty hunter. I'm just a lady with a fast ship trying to make a living, and I got word you might have some work for me."

We're not exactly sure, but Kiya figures it was during this conversation that Dad was marked by a sniper.

As Kiya said, there was a price on his head among the pirate planets. He was trying to make peace. Pirates don't like peace, as a general rule. They wanted him dead, but not just dead; captured, tortured, humiliated, and executed. Deader than dead.

I guess with all the visitors coming for Mom's funeral, someone slipped through security and managed to put a mark on Dad. A mark, by the way, is a tiny transmitter that's painlessly shot into a person's skin and can be monitored from anywhere in the galaxy. It's a quantum entanglement thing, but don't ask me how it works. I don't know, don't care.

Anyway, he said to Kiya, "I want to hire you to take me and my daughter, Nadir, to my parent's home on Caseri. Once I know she's settled, I want you to take me to the Council of Pirates. You can collect that bounty."

"I said I'm no bounty hunter."

"You'd be doing me a favor."

Kiya looked at him like he'd lost his mind, but then he let out a cough that sounded as fatal as his plan. Clearly, his space plague would kill him soon enough, so what difference would an execution make?

"There's a war coming," Dad said after he'd caught his breath. "If I can't stop it, maybe I can influence the aftermath."

"How so?"

"You ever hear of the Morian Treasure?"

"Just rumors and lies," said Kiya.

"The Warlord, Admiral Ghen, claims to be close to finding it. If he does, he'll have enough money and power to organize his own galactic war."

"He won't find it," said Kiya. "The Morian Treasure doesn't exist." She had a matter-of-fact manner that some might take as arrogance. I called it confidence.

"I know," Dad said, which made Kiya take notice. "Ghen uses the myth of the treasure to sustain his power with the Council of Pirates."

"You mean, 'Join me and you'll get your share of the treasure' thing?" said Kiya.

"Exactly. He'll raise a big enough armada whether he finds the treasure or not."

"So how do you fight a myth?"

"You create another one." Dad looked over at me. I think he knew I was listening, but they weren't talking about anything he and I hadn't already discussed. "I've dedicated my life to peace. It's time I dedicated my death as well."

"Your death?"

"I'm hoping for a very public execution."

I broke Dad's gaze to look over at Mom's grave. This was, without a doubt, the most awful day of my life, and it was about to get worse.

# ACKNOWLEDGEMENTS

As someone whose publishing career started by organizing an anthology, it's hard for me to believe it's been almost five years since our last. At one point, I even resigned myself to not launching another.

But I've always loved short stories – reading them, writing them, sharing them. And I've been fortunate to find other authors who enjoy them at least as much as I do.

I learned a long time ago that publishing can never be a solo-enterprise. This anthology would not have been possible without the wise counsel of fellow author friends. And in this case, it was especially important for me to communicate with science fiction writers. I am indebted to Vicki Weavil and Joyce Alton for their advice, and I think R.C. Lewis has inserted some gray matter of hers into my brain. At least I hope so! Every time I communicate with her about stories or editing, I feel like I learn something.

And a special thank you, also, to R.S. Mellette, whose stories have entertained me since he first sent me one for *Spring Fevers*. I'm proud to be launching his Dark Star Warrior series in the coming months. I believe 2020 will be a great year for the EBP herd.

Sound the trumpets!

# ABOUT THE AUTHORS

**Jon Fried** has collected his short stories into three books: stories about work and life in the corporate age, called *Transcendent Guide to Corporate America,* stories about romance and relationships, including "Primary Season (Love Red on Planet Blue)," called *Useless Guide to Modern Romance,* and stories in neither category called *Guide for the Unguidable*, which is also the name of his blog. He has published short fiction in several journals and e-zines, as well as feature stories on New Jersey culture and nightlife for *The New York Times*. One of his stories won a prize. One of his collections almost won a prize (third place). He wrote and produced many songs for a rock band he co-founded with his wife, Deena Shoshkes, called the Cucumbers, which released several recordings. Currently, he and Deena play in a six-piece mostly acoustic band called the Campfire Flies, which recently released its debut album. He is also working on a series of novels based on some colorful characters in his family tree.

**Kelly Heinen** holds a BA in English from Buena Vista University and an AAS in Broadcasting from Iowa Central Community College. When she's not writing, Kelly can be found working in radio, costuming, or slinging donuts at the local bakery. Kelly enjoys spending her spare time with family, her nieces Lyra, Norah, and Mackenzie, her cat Benvolio, and her boyfriend Scott. She enjoys reading, writing, and listening to and playing music, as well as working in her garden. She is dedicating her story in the *Flight* collection "to the memory of my mother, Jean Heinen, my grandmothers Marcella and Marie, and my muse, Jimmy. With special thanks, as always, to my best friends Amber, Meredith, Ronda, Scott, Ruth, and Cathy for always being there when I need them."

**R.S. Mellette** is a proud member of the Elephant's Bookshelf herd. Besides short stories in several EBP anthologies, Mellette has authored three EBP novels: *Billy Bobble Makes a Magic Wand* (2014), its sequel, *Billy Bobble and the Witch Hunt* (2016), and the upcoming debut novel in the Dark Star Warrior series, *The Morian Treasure*, which is scheduled for release from EBP in 2020. Outside of EBP, Mellette wrote the first web-to-television intellectual property, "The Xena Scrolls," for Universal Studio's *Xena: Warrior Princess*. He also has had various jobs from script coordinator to actor on *Blue Crush*, *Nutty Professor II*, *Looney Tunes: Back In Action*, *Star Trek: Enterprise*, *Days of Our Lives*, *Too Young The Hero*, and countless stage productions across the U.S.

**Robert Wayne McCoy** is the father of two and happily married. *The King of Ice Cream* was his first published novel by Five Star Press in 2004. It was a western-inspired story of modern-day gun-slinging Paladins and dark religious magic. Short story credits of note include "The Stuff of life to Knit You" (1995) "The Changing of the Guard" (1998) "The Lord of the Fantastic" in honor of Roger Zelazny, "The Splendour Falls," "The Youngest Horseman" (1999), "Lower Than The Angels," "The Company We Keep" (2003), "The Lady of the Owl Colored Eyes" (2013) in *Volted Tales*; and "Do Dead Psychic Smoke Cigarettes" (2014) *Winter's Regret*. Robert is writing a series of books that are linked, each novel a part of an epic canvas to be created over multiple books but with a unique twist. The nature of the story allows a reader to pick up any of the books and have that as the starting point. Through allusion and a free-flowing tale, the rest of the books fill in the blanks of the others; though each is also a standalone tale. The books he has written that are a part of a circular series are *The King of Ice Cream*, *Bound In Bitter Chains*, *The Game of Five*, and *The Lady of the Owl-Colored Eyes*. He is at work on the fifth book, tentatively titled *The Man Who Loved to Play in the Dirt*.

**Kathryn Rossati** is a U.K.-based author and poet who loves weaving tales of fantasy, sometimes with sci-fi or paranormal twists. As a writer on the autistic spectrum, she tends to write stories that have themes of social acceptance and equality, without the soap-box approach. Kathryn is the author of the magical middle grade trilogy, *Half-Wizard Thordric*; the stand-alone portal fantasy, *The Door Between Worlds*; and the young adult speculative fiction adventure, *The Origin Stone*. When not writing, she is Mother of Parrots and strolls around in dungarees quoting her favorite books and films.

**Matt Sinclair** knows that even if he had months to travel to Mars via ion-powered spaceship, he still wouldn't accomplish all his goals for Elephant's Bookshelf Press. An inveterate underachiever, he is happy that the publishing company has now published its fourteenth book, has its fifteenth and sixteenth in process, and is hoping to reach twenty books by the end of 2020.

All right, that last one probably won't happen, but he likes to dream. When not fashioning EBP out of whole cloth, he works as a journalist in New York City. *Flight* is his first anthology since the Mets last reached the World Series, which is just too damn long. We won't even discuss how long it's been since they won it all!

**N.B. Turner** is a young writer who is proud to have his first print publication with Elephant's Bookshelf Press. A Midwesterner by birth, Turner currently lives in northern Virginia and attempts to see the world for all its light and darkness with an honest eye and a good sense of humor, and he hopes to publish many more stories that show both in full form. He considers himself a literary student of Ray Bradbury, Flannery O'Connor, and Graham Greene and an admirer of Ottessa Moshfegh and John Le Carré.

Dark Star Warrior: The Morian Treasure
is coming in 2020 from Elephant's Bookshelf Press

Become a Dark Star Warrior!

Go to https://elephant-s-bookshelf-press.ck.page/557820aea9